THE MIND FROM
OUTER SPACE

ALSO BY EANDO BINDER

Adam Link, Robot
The Double Man
The Eando Binder MEGAPACK®
Enslaved Brains
The Forgotten Colony
The Impossible World
The Mind from Outer Space

THE SAUCER SERIES

Menace of the Saucers
Night of the Saucers

THE MIND FROM OUTER SPACE

EANDO BINDER

WILDSIDE PRESS

To Clifford Kornoelje, my first fan.

CHAPTER 1

"Eureka!" yelled a voice from Lab 1, with all the excitement Archimedes may have displayed over 2000 years ago.

Going down the hall on his weekly rounds of Serendipity Labs, Dr. Amos Clyde looked surprised, then hurried his pace into the door of Lab No. 1. A youthful scientist turned, brushing back a crew cut.

"What is it, Barton?" said Dr. Clyde, director of this series of labs and the brain-boys who ran them. "Why that melodramatic expression? Terribly out of date, you know...."

Barton shook his head. "It wasn't me, Doc. That creative cry came from Brains here."

"The computer?" frowned Clyde, dubiously. *Brains* stood for Binary Rapid Analog and Integral Nth-Power System.

"Yes," nodded Barton with a straight face. "As you remember, I was trying something new with it, opening all the circuits and programming it to invent anything it liked, just to see what would happen. Well, it came up with something startling...but let Brains tell you himself."

The giant high-speed computer ensemble had long ago been equipped with voice as well as tape and typewriter read-out. Barton pressed the "report" button. With its flat mechanical tones, the computer boomed out: "Today I invented a man!"

Clyde looked stricken and opened his mouth, but Brains was pouring out more brassy words. "You take oxygen, hydrogen, nitrogen, carbon, and various other elements and mix well in chemical combination until you get amino acids to form proteins and build up cells. Properly distributed, those cells make up an animate form with appendages and a head. Then add blood and a heart to pump it through the arteries, lungs to breathe in air, a sex organ, and a few more odds and ends, and you have a creature called man...."

Dr. Clyde heard the titter behind him. Crowding in the hallway beyond the door were most of the staff of Serendipity Labs with broad grins on their faces.

Clyde turned scarlet and turned accusingly on Barton. "You… you… It's all a joke on me. Barton, I'll…"

Again he was drowned out by Brains. "But this invention is to be rejected. The end product is utterly worthless."

Clyde relaxed. He had a group of wild intellects under him whose humor was equally wild. "All right, Barton," he said quietly, "you've had your fun." But a firm note rose in his voice as he went on. "However, it's hardly appropriate to use our busy computer for trivial pranks like that."

Barton shrugged. "That only used one millionth of Brains' capacity. All the other projects he's working on…let's see, thirty-four at present…are still clicking away smoothly." He pointed to the flashing banks of coded lights and spinning tapes down the row of cabinets.

Barton changed his tone. "However, Brains *did* invent a man when given only the basic raw data. It was a dry run for my new project, which is to give him free rein and see if he does come up with something unique. Something our human brains never thought of."

And that was the keynote of Serendipity Labs, Clyde reflected. To try any offbeat, unorthodox, harebrained experiments in all science fields and technologies. Serendipity—the unexpected, the random chance, the stroke of luck, the unplanned breakthrough.

Clyde winced a little, thinking of the name outside scientists often used scornfully for his pioneering group—the Blunder Boys, casting about in all directions and blundering into something new.

Yet it was paying off, he thought more pridefully as he made his way down the hall again. The appreciative group who had come to take in Barton's little joke had dispersed to their own labs and brain-beating problems.

In Lab No. 2, a stout, muscled man with a black patch over one eye and a heavy-jowled face looked the picture of a pirate of old. But along with the lilting name of Dr. Alloway Argyle, he had a sensitive mind that probed into unexplored regions of the nuclear microcosmos.

Growling his usual gravel-voiced greeting, Dr. Argyle reported on his pet project. "I've got the magnetic spin for the quark now and have its theoretical properties fairly well tabulated…"

"The quark…the quark," interposed Clyde a bit blankly.

"Oh, you know, the supposedly basic nuclear particle that makes up the electron, proton, neutron, hyperon, all the mesons, and the rest. But I'm on the track of something even more fundamental." He paused, his eyes shining like a buccaneer sighting a Spanish galleon loaded with gold.

Dr. Clyde waited expectantly.

"The Ultimaton, I call it," rasped Argyle's voice. "It may well make up the quark itself."

"Then it must be incredibly small," said Clyde. "How tiny is it?"

"It has no size at all."

Clyde stared. "What about weight?"

"No weight either."

"Magnetic moment?" ventured Clyde. "Electric charge?"

"None."

"No size, weight, magnetism, nor charge," said Clyde, suspiciously. "Is this another joke, like Barton pulled…?"

Argyle looked indignant, fixing the director with his one good eye blazing. "The Ultimaton may have one property no other nuclear particle has, one that places it in a unique category—it may be alive."

"Alive?" gasped Clyde.

"A living vibration," amended Argyle obscurely. "It may account for why inorganic or 'dead' matter can form living plants and animals. It may actually be the root of…."

His voice trailed away and he stood blank-faced, his mind wandering off into remote regions. As if leaving a sleeping person, Clyde made no further comment and tiptoed out. Sometimes Argyle stood that way for half a day and not even an exploding bomb could bring him back from the unknown realm of thought through which he was wandering and seeking.

In Lab No. 3, Dr. Clyde absent-mindedly said "Good morning" to the nude female figure standing within. Then he caught himself and flushed, not from embarrassment but for not remembering.

"My androids look real, eh?" chortled Dr. Allen Chumley, waving at the other nude figures of both men and women. "All synthetic flesh out of vats."

"You could at least clothe them," muttered Clyde. "Any further results in giving them intelligence?"

Chumley's fat body heaved out a mournful sigh. "No, not yet. But someday, somehow, I'll energize the gray plastic matter within their plastic skulls."

Leaving him sighing, Clyde went to Lab No. 4, to be greeted by a flood of profanity no truck driver could ever match. And yet the man within had an angelic face and poetic air.

"Don't ask me," snarled Dr. Ivan Yonah, standing beside a bulky electronic apparatus with a bubble-chamber, "if I've detected chronons yet, the units of time. They must be there in my bombardment of negative mesons but the cussword cussword cussword cussword…."

Clyde closed the door behind him with the string of imprecations rising to a grand crescendo of frustration. Clyde wished he had some frustration pills that you could hand out like aspirin for headaches. His intellectual prima donnas suffered the tortures of the damned twice over when their pet projects turned out wrong.

In Lab No. 5, a short man, almost of dwarf size, turned his oriental face toward Clyde and spoke in a high-pitched tone. "Axes, clubs, blowtorches, rifle bullets—any weapon you can name—has no slightest effect on the stuff. But a laser beam"—he pointed sadly at a hole in a square plate of steel-like material—"will drill through it in an hour."

"Too bad, Dr. Cheng," said Clyde. "Are you going to abandon the project?"

"No," snapped the scientist. "I can still try interlocking the atoms another way until I finally achieve my goal—indestructible matter."

Down the hall, Clyde checked into other labs. One where a Kelvin thermometer registered below absolute zero, proving there was a negative range of coldness never before suspected. In another lab the experimenter was barking like a dog, with a real dog cocking his head and answering, one of various attempts to set up communications with animals.

Other labs featured experiments in growing one-celled amoebas as big as washtubs, making objects vanish into and return from the fourth to the twenty-eighth dimensions, manipulating subtle forces akin to black magic, making amorphous matter dribble out of tanks of pure energy trapped therein, and some experiments Clyde did not even understand.

The director shook his head in wonder, continuing down the hall. A couple dozen hand-picked brains were under his wing, each a genius or something beyond. The Floyd Foundation, which had subsidized and launched this untried venture, had already seen the first of the rewards that came out—three new technological triumphs, including the gravity intensifier, five bombshell theories in cosmology of which one featured invisible stars, two biological breakthroughs with one being a cancer inhibitor if not cure, and a dozen more miscellaneous science steps ahead, topped by the ESP gauge that could detect involuntary thought transmissions from the brain though not read the actual messages.

Clyde was thinking of its creator as he entered Lab No. 11. *Thule W. Hillory—Psi Phenomena* read the lettering on the door. The first thing that met the eye was a big chart on the wall. One part of it showed the electromagnetic spectrum of gamma rays, X-rays, ultraviolet light, the optical octave, infrared rays, microwaves, radar, and radio.

The other chart, obviously an analogy, listed "mental octaves"—telepathy, clairvoyance, psychokinesis, precognition and retrocognition, psychogenesis, dreams, hypnosis, 6th sense hunches, and astral projection. Then, at the topmost end of the scale was a space with a question mark plus the words *free mind*.

Of all the Serendipity Labs roster of academic stars, Hillory was not a Ph.D. His formal education had been a ramble through several colleges and universities and a degree from none. But when interviewed and tested, he displayed an IQ that ran off the board. He was accepted by the Floyd Foundation screening board when he casually wrote down a formula that tied the alpha brain waves of human slumber into a waking state—the first known empirical link between the subconscious and conscious minds. Thereafter, in stature, he was, in their eyes, about three Ph.D.'s wrapped into one, with or without the scrap of paper conferring the title of "doctor" on him.

Yet Clyde could never get over the mild shock of seeing this amazing brain encased in a physical form that was hardly impressive.

Hillory was tall and thin, almost gaunt. His face was craggy and one shaggy eyebrow was permanently lifted above the other. He moved in jerks as if not fully in control of his body. His lips twitched constantly. His blond hair, cut short, stood out in bristles as if he were constantly charged with 50,000 volts. He walked in a slouch as if always passing under low doorways.

He was checking over notes with Merry Vedec, one of the many girl technicians hired by Serendipity Labs as aides to unburden the brain crew from routine tasks. Merry was no Miss America either, with irregular features and a somewhat slender, bosomless body. She looked the sexless female type—until you saw her enormous brown bedroom eyes, languid and heavy-lidded. Passion slumbered within her and subtly radiated its siren call to almost any man she looked at.

"How's the mind-over-matter bit going?" queried Clyde.

Hillory jerked around in his ungainly fashion. He formed a crooked smile of greeting with his twitching lips. Then a frown of frustration filled his face.

"It's more like matter-over-mind," said Hillory, his voice surprisingly melodious like an opera singer. "My brain matter is too dense to figure out where the mind lurks within my skull, or anybody else's."

Hillory picked up an odd-looking wire-mesh helmet and placed it on his head at a ludicrous angle. "This gizmo was supposed to separate my brain from my psyche. Free my pure mind." He grinned wryly. "All it did was give me a horrible headache never before matched on God's green earth. Super headaches now available! Straight from Serendipity Labs. Pah! The most useless invention in the world."

He tossed the helmet aside.

"Come on," Hillory added suddenly, grabbing the girl's hand. "I'll give you a motorcycle ride. Good way to clear the sticky cobwebs out of my head."

Merry nodded and went out with him. Dr. Clyde made no protest. His brainy brood had complete freedom of action with no restrictions. If they wanted to loaf or take a day off, it was their sole choice.

And the girl technician might be needed to take notes if inspiration abruptly struck him.

CHAPTER 2

The motorcycle with its two riders sped out of the parking lot and took the winding road up the hill. Looking back, one could see the sprawling low building that housed Serendipity Labs and its mental giants. Purely functional, it was a misshapen box set down among rolling hills at the western edge of New Jersey, looking out upon the majestic Delaware Water Gap over in Pennsylvania—a quiet setting with the main highway fourteen miles away and the nearest small township hidden behind the hills.

Merry hung onto Hillory's middle as he jerked the motorcycle around bends, just as he jerked his body around on foot. The cycle's muffled roar echoed at times from cliffsides as he headed toward a wilder section of the countryside that was sparsely populated.

"Too many bumps?" yelled Hillory as the pavement petered out and they jounced along a rough dirt road.

"No, go faster," sang out Merry gleefully. "I was a tomboy when I was a little girl and I've never gotten over it. This is cool, man."

Hillory gunned the motor until the motorcycle was more in the air than on the ground. They came down each time after a bump with jarring impact. Hillory glanced back admiringly at the girl's excited face, enjoying the physical punishment and its spice of danger. For now they rode alongside a steep ravine where disaster awaited if they ever careened into it.

Hillory snapped "hullo" and suddenly put on the brakes, so violently that the skid almost threw Merry off.

"Try again if you want to blow a tire," she said in ruffled good humor.

"I wasn't playing rough rider," said Hillory, pointing down into the ravine. "What's that?"

The girl peered down where his finger pointed. Through the shrubs and gnarled slope-clinging trees she caught a glint of something metallic.

Hillory was already scrambling down the slope and the girl followed gamely. "Might be a wrecked car," she said.

"No," barked Hillory, with an odd note of tenseness in his voice. "It's round and flat and silvery. And bigger. It's something else… something odd…"

Then, stopping on a rock overhang that gave a more unobstructed look below, they saw it clearly.

Merry gasped. "Why, it—it looks just like one of those flying saucers people keep reporting."

Hillory grunted and started downward again. They were scratched by brambles and panting from exertion by the time they reached the bottom of the ravine where the strange machine lay. It had obviously crashed here, for the lower part of the disc-shaped vehicle was crushed, and it lay at a slant on one edge.

"It still shines brightly," breathed Merry. "Must have crashed recently."

"No," denied Hillory, glancing around keenly. "The metal seems rustless, but notice the edges coated with moss and lichens, and how weeds have grown up into the smashed bottom openings. It's been here years, maybe centuries, who knows?"

Merry's eyes were round. She spoke with a gulp. "Do you suppose there's…*someone* in it? His body or his skeleton? Someone from…."

She made a sweeping eloquent wave, in awe, at the sky.

"From outer space, what else?" said Hillory matter-of-factly. "Let's go see."

Hillory stooped and crawled under the jagged broken edges of the saucer's bottomside. He straightened up and found himself in what had been the interior cabin, outfitted with various wall-panel gauges, dials, and indicators.

In the gloom, with sunlight cut off, he swept his eyes around and then started. Huddled in a corner against the wall was a skeleton. No, not exactly a skeleton of inner bones upon which flesh had been hung. It was an *outer* skeleton, like the chitinous armor of insects, *inside* of which the flesh had once existed but was now no more than a few dried shreds. The external skeleton was shaped more or less in manlike form, including the selfsame kind of skull humans had.

From what unthinkably remote star had he come? What bizarre kind of civilization existed there? And what had been his mission here on earth? Hillory shook his head at these unanswerable questions.

He peered closer, then, at the skeleton's bony hand, which clutched what seemed to be a scroll. Hillory was able to climb up on the undamaged flooring of the vehicle and crawl on hands and knees close to the dead alien's remains. A lingering stench of decay and rot almost made him retch. But he forced his stomach to quiet down and then carefully pulled the scroll out of the bony hand.

As he crawled back, Hillory could feel with surprise that it was not a scroll of paper he held. It was a thin metallic sheet rolled up. When he brought it out into the sunlight, he saw its bright silvery gleam. But it was heavy, too heavy to be aluminum or even tin foil. Must be iridium, platinum, osmium, something like that. Long-lasting, corrosion-resisting metals.

"What's that?" Merry was asking curiously.

Hillory told of the saucerman's skeleton and began unfurling the crinkly scroll. When one full side was exposed, they could see it was covered with strange symbols and markings all of which had been embossed on the metal itself. There had been no ink or dye to fade away through long stretches of time.

"Did the dead pilot come to earth," puzzled Hillory, "to deliver this message—if that's what it is?"

Merry peered closely and extended her finger to an "emblem" at the top. "Thule, it looks like three long bones crossing one another."

"Hmm," said Hillory. "Reminds me of something else…some other symbol or emblem on earth…but I can't place it."

"What does the message say?" asked Merry innocently.

Hillory gave her a withering look. "This language, if it is a language, was devised on a planet maybe a hundred or a thousand light-years away. It would have no slightest connection with any language on earth. And you expect me to translate it on the spot. What am I, a super-genius?"

"Yes, you are," said the girl sincerely. "But what I meant was just that I was *wondering* what it said, not for you to tell me. Do you think anybody could ever decipher it?"

'I wonder," said Hillory. "But Serendipity Labs can try. If they all look it over, some clues may come up allowing us to crack even a nonearthly code or language."

With some trepidation, he eyed the steep side of the ravine they would now have to climb. "Well, let's go."

Merry paused and froze, without turning. "Thule! I hear a noise behind us…*footsteps!*"

They both whirled, gasping. The alien's skeletonized body was emerging from under the wrecked saucer. It straightened up and creakingly moved toward them, its bony arms raising and stretching toward them.

"It came alive!" screamed Merry, "as if it wants the scroll back that you took…" She ended in a bubbling moan of terror.

Hillory looked dumbly at the scroll in his hand. Could it really be that? He grabbed the girl's hand and started desperately to scramble up the slope. But their feet slipped under loose rubble.

Hillory caught a whiff of the horrible stench close behind him, and then a bony hand seized the scroll and wrested it from his hand.

"It's impossible," Hillory breathed. "An alien's skeleton could no more move than a human's fleshless bones."

"Maybe not," moaned Merry, eyes wide as if viewing a nightmare, "but it's running away with the scroll."

Hillory galvanized into action. He picked up a boulder as big as a football, brought it up over his head, then heaved it with all his power. The stone caught the ambling skeleton squarely in the back. There was a multiple cracking sound and the whole bony structure flew apart, scattering pieces for ten yards. The scroll dropped to the ground.

Hillory ran and snatched it up, then began pulling the girl up the slope. She kept glancing back at the pile of bones. "How could a lifeless skeleton move?" she moaned several times. "It's like witchcraft…."

"Shut up," panted Hillory, as they laboriously crawled up the ravine's steep slope. "Forget it. The important thing is we've got the scroll."

Reaching the top of the slope at last, they looked back, perspiring and gulping air into their heaving lungs. After one last look at the wrecked flying saucer and the scattered bone structure in the ravine, they turned toward their motorcycle, leaning against a tree.

And then the motorcycle moved, by itself.

Turning white, both Hillory and the girl stood in paralyzed astonishment. The engine had not started but still the motorcycle, as if imbued with a life of its own, gathered speed and came straight for them.

"No chance to run, or get behind a tree," gasped Merry, with only seconds to go before the impact.

"I've got an idea," rasped Hillory, at the same time hurling the scroll aside to land at the foot of a massive tree trunk. The motorcycle immediately swerved toward the scroll, starting to slow down. But its momentum was too great to be checked in that short space. There was a thud as the cycle's front tire struck the tree trunk, and the vehicle bounced back several yards, to topple and lie inert. It did not move anymore.

"Quick," said Hillory, "follow me, Merry. The cycle's undamaged." After kicking the motor to life, Hillory gunned it away with Merry clinging behind him.

"Do you think," screeched Merry above the wind's roar, "that it was the dead alien's…uh…s*pirit* that animated his skeleton and then our motorcycle?"

"An interesting theory," returned Hillory, "except that it sounds like sheer metaphysical rot. Maybe we'll solve that weird mystery sometime, but the main thing is to tackle this scroll—a message, perhaps from some faraway world. The biggest thing since…well, for a long, long time."

* * * *

"Hen scratching," grunted Argyle. "Hieroglyphics. But we don't have an interstellar Rosetta Stone. Impossible to translate."

He handed the foil sheet to Dr. Cheng. It passed down the line. They were all assembled in the computer lab. One after another the Serendipity scientists looked over the "writing" and shrugged.

"No slightest clue to tie it in with the meaning of the symbols or words," declared Dr. Chumley.

Hillory swung on the computers master. "Barton, can Brains decipher it?"

"How would I program it to Brains?" Barton asked dubiously. "If we knew what one letter or number was, it might be a hook allowing Brains to crack the rest."

"But you said you had been 'training' Brains to cook up new projects or discoveries of his own," said Hillory. "Why not just run it through the computer without any instructions?"

"Say, it's worth a try," mused Barton, stroking his blond handlebar mustache. Suddenly he snatched up the foil sheet and inserted it into the scanning slot. Then he simply flipped over the main toggle switch marked "Analyze."

"I'll have to temporarily switch off work on the other projects we fed into Brains," he said apologetically to his colleagues. "He may need all his capacities to handle this brain-buster."

The others nodded, some reluctantly, and Barton flipped over other studs to the off position. Now the computer's banks of lights began to blink on at a furious pace, and every tape in the system began spinning.

Barton whistled, looking at the central gauges. "Brains never met anything like this before. He's turning on every analyzing circuit he's got, searching every memory bank, and pouring in every transistorized unit. He's putting on full steam."

They fidgeted for the next half-hour. Dr. Clyde waved at the waiting scientists. "The rest of you might as well get back to your labs. We'll inform you when and if Brains gives the answer."

The others were glad to go, leaving only Clyde, Barton, the girl, and Hillory to fidget more time away.

Clyde turned his soft blue eyes on Hillory. "As if we didn't already have enough king-size research headaches here, you had to bring in a mind-cracking riddle from outer space." His voice sounded half-annoyed.

Hillory paused in his jerky pacing of the room. "If you found a chunk of gold one yard across, would you ignore it or bring it in as a vast treasure?"

"Please," Clyde hastened to assure him. "I wasn't blaming you for this, Hillory." A sudden thought struck him. "Hmm. If it *is* a message from another world, and *if* Brains can translate it, think of the prestige and glory Serendipity Labs would gain. International honors…Nobel prizes…science service medals…."

"Forget it," broke in Barton, shattering Clyde's bubble. "Brains just gave his answer."

Barton had read a coded tape, but now he flipped a replay switch and the computer's artificial voice boomed out. "The sheet bears markings suggesting a message, but no such language is known on earth. No characteristics of language structure remotely similar to earth's system of worded thoughts. The scroll's symbols are untranslatable."

As if to punctuate his pronouncement, Brains flipped the metal-foil sheet out of the reject slot. It thudded to the floor.

Barton picked it up slowly and handed it mutely to Hillory. Hillory stared at it, biting his lips.

"Can't you feed it back into Brains with some sort of programming, like try comparing it with every known dead language…."

"Obviously," returned Barton scathingly, "Brains already did that. He also used every system of code-breaking known to the FBI, CIA, Interpol, and what have you. We originally poured that basic data into his memory banks along with the Encyclopedia Britannica, every major science book written, the essence of all philosophy, religion, and politics. Then he was also fed…."

"Never mind," said Hillory wearily, jerking up his hand. "You're saying that if Brains can't chew it apart, nobody else on earth can."

"Right," nodded Barton. "Sorry, old man."

Hillory turned away with the metal scroll, his tall gaunt body stooped in disappointment. Merry followed him, sympathy in her face.

* * * *

"It's 3 a.m." yawned Merry, tossing another scribbled page aside to join the heap on the floor. "I've filled three notebooks, boiled up four pots of coffee, and worn out six pencils, not to mention my fingers. And I've got the world's worst case of writer's cramp."

Hillory mumbled something. For hours he had dictated, trying one or another approach at substituting earth words in the scroll and working from there. The serendipity method, blind groping, in the hopes of stumbling on the golden key.

"How can you hope to beat a computer?" said Merry, rather sharply. "Aren't you overestimating your own brain-power?"

"Brains doesn't operate on serendipity," said Hillory. "He starts from some logical premise and builds up an orderly structure of analysis, all neat and correct. He doesn't know how to put square-peg facts into round-hole receptacles and come up with something fantastic and unknown. But the 'scatter-brained' human mind has the unique ability—or curse, perhaps—to think *irrationally*. The road, sometimes, to the serendipity pot-of-gold."

He lapsed into a brooding silence, staring at the scroll intently. "But I swear," he began again, "that there is something just beyond my reach in these mouse tracks. A clue, a key, an insight…if I could only grab hold of it."

He picked up a magnifying glass and peered at alien symbols. "Some of them are tiny drawings it seems. One of them looks like a mountain. It makes me think of something…."

His leaning chair slammed to the floor. "By the blue gods," he hissed, "suppose it's not dealing with a language or words, but with coordinates, degrees, areas, distances, and locations?"

He bent over with his magnifying glass again. "One symbol is repeated over and over again, not like the common letter 'e' in language, but more like…aha…d*egrees*!"

He jerked around toward Merry. "What if it's a *map*?"

CHAPTER 3

"Dragging a man out of bed at 6 a.m. is sheer effrontery," grumbled Jim Barton. He forced open his sleepy eyes to glare at Hillory as he came out of his dormitory room tucking his shirt in his trousers. "In plain words it stinks."

"You won't complain when you hear about this," said Hillory, waving the rolled-up metal sheet. "I've had an inspiration. It's not a message per se. It's a map."

"Map?" Barton looked blank, stroking his somewhat crumpled mustache to even it out.

Hillory went on eagerly, jerking the words out. "Yes. Or rather, a chart. I want Brains to analyze it from that viewpoint."

They reached the computer room, and Hillory spread the metal sheet flat. "If you look closely, you can see faint lines we didn't notice before. They look like geographical configurations that might exist right here on earth. Here, use this."

He handed Barton a magnifying glass.

"Hm," said Barton, squinting through it. "Does look somewhat like cartography. You may have hit the jackpot. I'll program Brains to make like it deals with degrees, radii, great circles, and areas."

Sleepiness forgotten, he began energetically to tap a keyboard that translated worded instructions into computerese. "This'll take some time," he flung over his shoulder. "Rustle up some Java."

Hillory nodded and ambled down the hall to the kitchen. Nobody was on duty so he had to poke around in the cabinets for a jar of freeze dried coffee, to which he added boiling hot water in two mugs. He brought them steaming to where Barton still pecked at his keys, pausing at times in thought.

"There's a glitch in this," he mused, between gulps of the scalding coffee. "The makers of this map didn't happen to go to school on earth, so why would they have a circle divided into 360 degrees? It could be 250 or 600 or anything. Hmm, I'll have to tell Brains to look for the pi value first and deduce the system of degrees. Same with linear dimensions and distances, assuming this map refers to earth. Brains will have to do some tall interpreting."

"But if the chart is based on earthly topography," put in Hillory, "Brains will have some basis of comparison with our measurements."

"That's the big white hope," admitted Barton, jabbing at keys steadily. "A language with no common reference points was hopeless. But a set of directions to physical places right here on earth's surface immediately brings in common denominators."

He turned with his finger poised over a red button. "Now feed the alien chart into the slot."

Hillory obeyed and Barton jabbed the button. Lights began to blink as Brains accepted its new assignment. Barton flipped the voice feed-out.

"Do you reject the problem, stated in new terms?"

"No. It could be solvable."

"Could be? What kind of an answer is that?" Barton was puzzled. Brains had always before stated things in unqualified yeses and no's. "Listen, Brains, is it affirmative or negative that you will solve it?"

"Probably affirmative," came back in mechanical tones.

"First time I knew Brains to be cautious," said Barton in an aside to Hillory. "Guess it hinges on whether he can successfully pin down any point on earth with the alien designations."

To Brains he said, "How long will this brain buster take you?"

The computer had a built-in timer that revealed in advance how long any problem would take to be solved. The answer flashed on a lighted screen—5 HOURS, 7 MINUTES, 23 SECONDS.

"Whew. Want some aspirin?" asked Barton.

"No comment."

Barton turned to Hillory with widened eyes. "Brains never took that long to crack any other mental nut. It's equivalent to a scientist saying a lab experiment will take him forty years."

"Five hours," grunted Hillory, obviously impatient. He threw himself into a chair. "May as well get some rest, I suppose. I've been up all night. But I won't be able to sleep, I know." Ten seconds later he was snoring. Barton grinned, checked the circuits, then sprawled in another chair with a deep sigh.

The computer labored away silently, its blinking lights accelerating into a frenzied sequence as it wrestled with the knottiest problem any cybernetic device on earth had ever been given.

Something nudged Hillory's sleeping brain, warning him to wake up. Opening his eyes he saw a huge naked man standing over Barton and pulling a rope tight around his neck. Only stifled gasps came from Barton as his face purpled and his eyes bulged. His flailing arms and legs began to go limp.

Hillory stared in horror, as if in a nightmare. Then, snapping wide awake, he hurled his lanky form forward, catching the nude assailant around the legs and throwing him to the floor. This loosened the rope around Barton's neck and his lungs heaved in air.

The naked man quickly leaped to his feet and turned on Hillory, grabbing him around the middle with two arms and squeezing powerfully. Hillory's breath wheezed out as his lungs caved in. But then he put both hands under the man's chin and shoved violently, breaking his bear-hug hold.

Hillory then slammed his big fist into the naked man's face with all the power of his boxing champ days in college. Without any expression or sound, the man fell flat and lay still.

Allen Chumley s fat face poked in the door. "All right. Which of you jokers swiped one of my androids?" Then his eyes popped as he saw Hillory reviving Barton and the nude form sprawled on the floor.

"Your android came in here and tried to strangle Barton, then finish me off," grunted Hillory.

"But that's impossible," gurgled Chumley, rushing to kneel at the android's side and rubbing his wrists anxiously. "Petunia here wouldn't hurt a fly. His rudimentary cortex can only handle simple orders, and I didn't order him to attack you."

Barton had recovered and was rubbing his neck tenderly. "Maybe not, but that hunk of lab-made meat turned killer. You'd better have him destroyed, Chumley."

"No, he's harmless," muttered Hillory.

"Harmless?" blazed Barton angrily. "After he nearly choked me to death?"

"It wasn't him," Hillory went on. He pointed to Chumley who was leading the android, now docile, by the hand out of the door. "It was something else that…." Hillory pondered how he could explain and began again.

"Barton!" Hillory was interrupted as Dr. Clyde rushed in, concern all over his face. "I just saw Chumley in the hall and heard of that weird attack by the android. Are you all right?"

Barton rubbed his neck with a grimace. "Yes, just some bruised skin. But I'll always know how it feels to be hanged on the scaffold."

"Go to the infirmary at once," said Clyde. "You must be checked by the doctor."

"Forget it, I'm all right," insisted Barton, lighting a cigar. But his hands were trembling now, from the reaction to his unsettling experience.

"I insist," said Clyde. With a shrug, Barton turned for the door. "Let the doc check me over then. But I'm going to be back before Brains gives his answer to the alien map."

"Alien *map*?" echoed Clyde when Barton had gone.

"Sorry, chief," Hillory smiled lamely. "Guess I should have informed you of my brainstorm." Hillory then told the surprised director of his inspiration. "We'll have the answer soon from Brains," he finished, "as to whether we're on the right track."

Hillory's face became serious. "But before that, I think there is something you all ought to know." He and Merry had not told the others, by common consent, of their experiences with the walking skeleton and murderous motorcycle. Now it had to be told.

"What should we know?" queried Clyde, puzzled.

"Let's wait until Barton returns from the checkup. I'm sure the doctor will release him shortly. And would you please call in Chumley. You can inform the rest of the staff later." Hillory noticed the puzzled look in Clyde's eye. "Believe me, it's important, chief."

"If you say so," nodded Clyde. He strode to where a telephone and intercom box stood on a table. He flipped the intercom's stud for Chumley's lab, telling him quietly to come.

Meanwhile, Merry Vedec came bustling in. "Thule," she said anxiously. "I slept late and I just heard about what happened. Did that horrible android hurt you? Was it like the skeleton and…"

Hillory took her hand and drew her aside. "Yes, and I'm going to tell the story in a moment. The rest have a right to know." His face became brooding. "We may all be in danger while that alien map is in our hands."

"Is it really a map?" asked Merry eagerly. "Was your hunch right?"

"Brains will give his answer in about 20 minutes." Barton came in at that moment. "Doc said I'm a roughneck," he announced flippantly. "Or toughneck, to be exact. No more than some lacerated skin." He stared around in surprise, suddenly noticing the others. "Why the big welcoming committee?"

"I've got something to tell all of you," said Hillory, drawing himself up and facing the small group. "The android didn't suddenly turn killer. Something entered him—*animated* him."

At their surprised murmurs, Hillory went on to tell of how the saucer skeleton and motorcycle had both menaced himself and Merry.

At the end, they were all looking stunned. "But what kind of strange force could make inanimate objects move like that?" whispered Barton.

"I don't know," admitted Hillory, his dark eyes brooding. "It might be some kind of intelligent entity that is invisible, even intangible, with the power to 'enter' objects and exercise kinetic force."

"Rot," scoffed Barton. "Anyway, why would it attack us here?"

"To get hold of that metal-foil map," said Hillory softly. "It failed to get the map away from Merry and me. So it tried here again."

"Sounds weird," said Barton with a shiver. "Some kind of ghost or spirit haunting us for an alien message."

"Not the traditional phantom," denied Hillory. He hesitated then blurted it out. "A *mind*. A disembodied alien mind from outer space, one that is determined to get that metal map away from us."

Clyde stared. "Now surely you don't mean a...a *pure mind*?"

"A free mind," amended Hillory, slowly. "You know of my psi experiments where I've charted the psychic factors in the human mentality, all the way from hypnotism and dreams to ESP. I can't go into detail here but there is strong empirical evidence that the mind itself is completely independent of the physical brain and can be separated from it. I've been trying to do it myself but haven't yet succeeded."

He waved at Barton. "Apparently our alien visitor did succeed and was able to animate the android. Become its mind, so to speak. Psychokinesis must have come into play, of course—the mental ability to move matter."

"Strange," muttered Chumley, who had listened intently. "I've been unable to activate the plasto-brains of my androids. Yet an alien mentality was able to do so and take over control of Petunia."

"That's all pretty much in the paranormal range," said Clyde shrewdly. "How sure are you that you've guessed right, Hillory?"

"I'm not sure at all," admitted Hillory, jerking up his hands. "Call it a hunch—which is also one of my charted psi characteristics. But this much I can say." He stared at the group somberly. "Assuming my theory of a free alien mind lurking among us is true, were all in danger—everyone at Serendipity that has anything to do with the metal map. The alien mentality, invisible to us, can enter other objects of any unexpected type. It may attack again and again. Obviously, it considers the metal map very important and it will use any means to wrest it away from us."

Clyde looked stricken. "A ghastly unseen killer stalking Serendipity Labs," he quavered, glancing fearfully over his shoulder. "This is terrible. I'm responsible for all of your lives. What will we do about it?" He was appealing to Hillory.

"Let's not press the panic button," Hillory said, but feeling a cold chill down his spine. "I was thinking about it before Barton returned. After we hear what Brains has to say, I'll carry out a plan I have in mind—to trap the mind-entity."

"Trap something invisible and intangible?" snorted Chumley.

Hillory was about to say more when a bell rang.

"The five hours and 7 minutes are up," said Barton, galvanized into action and running to his computer controls. "Brains is ready with his answer as to whether the metal scroll is a map or not."

All of them tensed with wonder. Hillory forgot to breathe.

With something of a dramatic gesture and unconsciously stroking his mustache, Barton pressed the button for voice read-out. The computer's flat tones sounded out. "The alien markings on the metal scroll are sections of a geographical chart, based on the topographical features of the planet Earth."

Hillory cheered silently. The others glanced at him in admiration for his ingenious insight into the mystery.

"A system of coordinates is used," went on the computer, "that uses a circle divided into 99 degrees, plus linear measurements analogous to kilometers and other metric units. From this, it can be determined that certain definite spots on earth are marked off as being significant."

The computer stopped, waiting for questions.

"Significant in what way?" demanded Barton.

"There are four such spots marked around the world. It would appear that something is hidden or buried at each spot."

Hillory and Barton jerked their eyes at each other, the same stunning thought instantly coming up.

"A treasure map," breathed Barton. "As if space pirates from some remote world hid their priceless loot on earth in different places." He shook his head in self-reproof at the bizarre thought. "Poppycock. It can't be storybook twaddle like that."

"Maybe not," agreed Hillory, "but it does seem as if *someone* from outer space did visit earth, perhaps long ago, and did conceal *something* at various earthly sites. What that something or somethings are, we can only find out by digging them up...."

He swung to the computer mike. "Tell me, Brains. Where is one of the marked locations?"

"This has not yet been figured out," returned the cybernetic mastermind.

"Why not?" snapped Barton.

"You didn't ask me."

Barton threw an imaginary bomb at the machine. "All right, smarty. So work out one of the four locations. How long will it take?"

23 MINUTES, 7.6 SECONDS read the lighted sign.

"Duck soup, eh?" grinned Barton. "Now that Brains has the basis of comparison between alien and earth measurements, he has an easy job so to speak. But still brain-twisting. I imagine he will have to scan each net of those fine lines to find some recognizable coastline or land mass on earth and go on from there."

Dr. Clyde was mopping his brow. "This is all so...overwhelming. So incredible." His face suddenly lighted up. "Actually, it's the biggest tiling Serendipity Labs has ever stumbled on. Interstellar treasure—"

"Whoa," said Hillory, jerking up a hand. "We don't know that. It's sheer guesswork. We can assume that something important to *aliens* is hidden at each spot, but we can hardly extrapolate as to what it is. It may be utterly worthless in earthly eyes."

"I'm no romantic nincompoop," returned Clyde, testily. "I meant 'treasure' in another sense. *Any* artifact from another civilization in space—even a two-headed spoon they eat with—would, of course, be a priceless find. In fact, mere gems or gold ingots would be a disappointment. The *things* of an extraterrestrial culture would be the real treasure."

CHAPTER 4

Clyde had put into words what all of them felt. The growing excitement at the thought of unearthing artifacts or relics that came from an alien civilization of some remote stellar system of planets. They all waited impatiently now for Brains to speak up. Pacing the floor, Barton and Hillory collided with one another and looked at each other in surprise.

Finally, the time limit was up and Barton pressed the voice button. Their faces collectively fell as the words boomed out.

"Unable to trace any of the four spots. The geographical markings and drawings do not seem to fit earth at all."

"Liar," spat out Barton, his mustache twitching angrily. "You told us before it did refer to earth topography. Explain your inconsistency—and it had better be good or I'll pour glue in your works." The others had to smile. Barton had formed an almost human rapport with his cyber partner and treated it like a sometimes recalcitrant servant.

"An anomaly does exist," reported Brains, in imperturbable tinny tones. "Analysis of the alien coordinates clearly showed it was a world the size of earth and having precisely one-g gravity, plus magnetic poles at the correct approximate positions. It would be unlikely for any other world to duplicate these conditions to as many decimal points. Yet upon trying to locate any one of the four spots, starting from a stated baseline, the data became erratic."

"Crazy. Wild. A world like earth and yet not like earth," breathed Barton, knocking his forehead. Hillory looked like someone who had fallen into a dark pit with no ray of light penetrating.

"A world not like earth," spoke up Merry Vedec in her lilting voice, "because it *changed* through the ages."

"That's it," yelped Hillory, coming out of his dark pit. "The saucer in which we found the document was ancient. The map refers to *prehistoric* earth, when the continents and seas and mountains were all different. We just have to get maps the geographers have worked out for prehistoric earth."

"But *which* prehistoric earth?" said Dr. Clyde quickly. "If you go back to Cambrian times, it's totally different from Jurassic times. Each age featured a far different face for earth. How do we choose?"

Hillory almost felt like hating Clyde. An enormous barrier now stood in their way. An air of gloom fell over them smotheringly.

"Wait a minute," said Barton, his voice lifting. "Simple. We date the saucer which held the scroll. Not carbon dating, of course, but whatever works with metal."

"No good," said Hillory. "The occupants of the saucer came with the scroll as if to find the treasure, to call it that. But who *made* the scroll and how much earlier? The ones who hid the treasure on earth might have done so centuries or thousands of years before. We're dealing now with cosmic stretches of time. So the answer is to date the scroll itself. But who—?"

"Yonah," said Clyde. "Ivan Yonah. His work on the chronon, or basic unit of time, has included all subatomic particles and all forms of radioactive breakdown of atoms."

Barton took the metallic scroll out of the computer, and they all strode down the hall to Yonah's lab. Long before they reached it, they heard the stream of smoking oaths from his open door.

"These cussword bubble-chamber tracks are no cuss-word cuss-word good," he was storming. The handsome man with angelic features glared at the visitors. "And what do you cussword people want?"

"Please," admonished Clyde. "There is a lady present."

"Merry?" snorted Yonah. "She taught me some of my best swear words, in five languages. Well, what's the cussword pitch?"

Hillory handed over the scroll with a short briefing on what had transpired. Finally he said, "Can you date it by radioactive techniques?"

Yonah turned the metal-foil sheet over and over in his hands. "The cussword stuff is osmium. Only way to date it is by measuring the residual radioactivity left in its thorium impurities—if it has any cussword impurities."

Hillory shuddered at that. "How long will it take?"

"Oh, several days, after I finish my current bubble-chamber work for a clue to the chronon."

"Days?" groaned Hillory. "Listen, do it right away."

"Sir?" said Yonah, drawing himself up indignantly and looking noble. "Drop my work for your cussword chasing of rainbows? I'll get at it tomorrow then, maybe."

"You will please get at it right now," said Clyde quietly, stepping forward.

"I cussword won't," growled Yonah.

"Yes, you will," barked Clyde, his goatee bristling. "It's a cussword *order*."

Yonah was so astonished at the mild-mannered director using an oath that his mouth hung open. "Well, if you put it *that* way," he chuckled, "I'll start right now."

"Wait," said Hillory in dismay, holding the osmium foil sheet. "This can't be dated by any radioactive method. It isn't *earthly* osmium. It's osmium from some other world that may have been formed sooner or later than earth in cosmological terms, maybe by millions of years. That would make its rate of thorium decay entirely different from a specimen of our osmium."

"You would think of that," said Barton, as if peeved at Hillory.

"But he's right, of course," agreed Yonah, looking disappointed. "Sorry I can't help. I doubt anyone can. But try Argyle, anyway."

They all trooped disconsolately to Lab No. 2 where Alloway Argyle, with his black eye-patch, looked like a pirate in disguise. His thick lips twisted almost malevolently in contrast to the cultured voice and words that came out. "Gentlemen? And the lady? How can I serve you?"

Hillory synopsized the story and held out the alien scroll. "Radioactive dating won't work," he said. "Is there any other method possible?"

"Yes, I think so." Argyle heaved his big body into a chair and spoke leisurely. "This will take a bit of explaining. Besides the embossed markings on the scroll, there are engraved markings. So my method would be to measure how much the etched lines in the metal map have filled up." At their blank stares, he went on. "Any material—even rock or glass or steel or any metal—tends to *flow* through a long enough period of time. Think of scratching a groove in soft wax. Come back a year later, and that groove will be partly filled in as the pressure of the side walls forces material inward."

He waved the heavy foil of alien metal. "Now in the case of osmium, you have to allow thousands or tens of thousands of years for the slightest appreciable filling of the groove."

"But that does no good," objected Hillory, "if you don't know how deep or wide that groove was originally, when the aliens scratched their chart on it."

"Not so," returned Argyle promptly. "When you scratch any hard surface with a sharp instrument, a groove is formed with ridges at the two sides. And there happens to be a constant that applies to any and all cut grooves. It's a ratio between its depth and width on the one hand, and the height of the ridges on the other hand. It will apply to the extraterrestrial osmium as well. All osmium in the universe, whether from some mine in Orion or some backyard junkpile on Betelgeuse—Betel-*juice*, you know—is chemically identical with local osmium. Besides, the groove-ridge ratio holds for any material from here to the next galaxy and beyond. It's a physical not chemical constant, relating to pressures and the slow movements of displaced atoms."

"Have you ever used this so-called dating method before?" asked Barton suspiciously.

Argyle's piratical face looked ferocious. "My dear skeptic. My first project here at Serendipity Labs, before my pursuit of the noble quark, was a study of universal principles of elemental atoms throughout the cosmos. It was then I applied my groove-ratio formula to the 'flow' of scratched metals. As a test, I dated a meteorite that way, analyzing its markings. My figure came out within 1 per cent of the estimate of meteorite specialists."

"I apologize," said Barton in visible relief.

"Then," growled Argyle, "let's get on with the dating process."

"How long will it take?" said Hillory, wincing at the thought of perhaps days for such a delicate operation.

"Oh, my meson microscope will easily magnify every detail of the grooves so that I can quickly determine how long ago the etched lines were first made. Say about three hours?"

Hillory looked happy. He took Merry's hand. "Meanwhile, let's visit the library and dig up all the ancient maps of earth through geological ages. We'll need them when Argyle gives his verdict."

The librarian on duty led Hillory and the girl to the chart room fairly well supplied with the necessary past-age maps of earth, as its surface was twisted and torn and rearranged constantly through violent upheavals.

Looking at the successively older maps, Merry made a face. "The farther back you go, the less earth's surface resembles anything we know today. There were flooded continents, mountain ranges being born or disappearing, or even a time when all the land masses of earth were together and slowly pulled apart. It's like an alien world way back there."

Hillory was just as depressed. "If the dating is anything older than the Pliocene Epoch a million years ago, we've had it. In the Pliocene, earth was roughly like it is today except for some surface changes made by several ice ages. But prior to that there would have been no landmark known today, such as Mount Everest or the Great Lakes. It would be hopeless to find any spot on the map in a younger and completely altered earth."

He gathered a sheaf of maps. "We'll take only those from the Pliocene onward into the Pleistocene and Neolithic eras. If Argyle's dating is in this range, we're in business."

As they went down the hall, Merry's brown eyes turned somberly to Hillory. "Thule, about that…that 'poltergeist' who animates dangerous things and tries to kill us? It's so eerie, the way it makes lifeless things move and act like killers. And how can we guess what form the killer will take next? He may attack again and again…till he gets us. Can you really trap it somehow?"

"I think I can," said Hillory hopefully. "Right after we pinpoint the four spots on the map—if we do—we'll set up the mind-trap."

Back at Argyle's lab, the scientist was grinning like a pirate who had just looted a shipload of gold. "Got your dating, son."

Hillory waited breathlessly.

CHAPTER 5

"The osmium foil sheet was etched 34,675 years ago, give or take 10 years, and not a year more," said Argyle firmly.

In joy, Hillory began riffling through the maps he had brought along. "Great. That's practically modem times. Hmm, that would be just before the Grcat Icc Age of 25,000 years ago, and earth would look like this."

He held up a map that was strange at first glance. But then a second glance clearly showed the rough outlines of the continents, with various inner areas flooded. Conversely there was a land bridge between Alaska and Siberia, and also from the Malayan peninsula to the Indonesian Isles. The shape of Europe was queerly distorted and Asia looked lopsided. But all modern mountain ranges were in existence and most coastlines had permanently formed.

"Like a surrealistic version of earth today," said Hillory. "But the four spots chosen to bury or hide things, by the aliens, would still exist today with very little change." He waved thanks to Argyle and was already racing to the computer lab, followed by Merry who picked up the other maps he had flung aside.

Barton looked at the map Hillory held up, stroking his mustache reflectively. "Not bad. What I'll do is feed this data to Brains, giving him a broad view of earth's surface configuration as of 35,000 years ago. From that he ought to be able to match it with the alien map."

An hour later he finished tapping out his programmed code, and again fed the metal-foil sheet into the computer, with instructions to find any one of thc four spots. The time screen flashed—11 MINUTES, 36 SECONDS.

"A breeze," grinned Barton. "Yet it only takes 10 minutes on the average to solve the toughest research problems fcd into it from Serendipity Lab experiments. This whole alien map bit is a plenty tough nut to crack."

It was late afternoon now, and Hillory was dog-tired from his sleepless night and the fast-paced events of the day. He spent the 11 minutes munching down sandwiches that Merry had quietly brought him, along with steaming hot coffee.

He kept glancing at his watch, in between, staring as if it had stopped or slowed down somehow. But at last the bell clanged. The word had gone around and Argyle was there, also Chumley and Dr. Clyde. All of them were caught up in the fantastic wonder of a "treasure map" from outer space, made before civilization had dawned on earth.

Barton had switched on the voice read-out, and Brains almost seemed to have a triumphant inflection in his flat tones. "Based on the map of earth's surface some 35,000 years ago, the alien chart now can be integrated with it, in rough fashion. Two spots were scanned but came out indecisively. However, the third spot became pinpointed as the tip of Mount Everest."

Hillory, somewhat giddy, did a little jig.

Barton was more practical. "Brains," he asked, "those two undetermined spots—can you pinpoint them with more work?"

"Affirmative—nearly."

Barton raised his eyebrows and even his mustache twitched. "And the final spot?"

"It will be even more difficult to pinpoint. Since the map of earth 35,000 years ago is only theoretical, there are certain discrepancies that do not match well with the alien map. But with a different approach via analogue techniques, I may be able in time to reconcile the two maps and name the spots." A pause. "Or, I may not."

Barton reached over and patted the shiny main cabinet of the computer complex. "You'll do it, old boy." He turned. "Anyway, we've got one spot that we can mark X on the map. Wonder why the aliens chose the tip of Mount Everest?"

"Because it's the highest mountain on earth," supplied Hillory. "Then and now. We can assume the other spots are also unique or prominent on earth. After all, if aliens were burying things on a strange new world, they would pick the most outstanding planetary features, to make the later job of digging them up easier."

Barton was shaking his head. "But who made the map? What did they hide here? Why have 35,000 years passed before the treasure map showed up? Why was it in the hands of flying saucer people? There's a whole lot of pieces of this jigsaw puzzle missing, if you ask me."

"All in good time," spoke up Dr. Clyde, moving forward. "I've been wondering what to do if the map was analyzed successfully. It becomes a big thing now, bigger than we are. I suppose I should turn the whole thing over to the government...."

"No." The word shot out from Hillory. His eyes held a gleam. "Look, I found the scroll-map. Let me finish the job—at least till the first spot is visited. Then we'll know more about what this mystery leads to. As of now, we could only give the government a vague lead. And you know all the red tape that would wrap itself around the project before they acted on it. *Why not keep this as a sort of top-secret project of Serendipity Labs?*"

Hillory glanced around and saw approval in all their eyes, except for Clyde. "But how," he said doubtfully, "can you or anybody here reach Mount Everest? If we request a special plane or helicopter or expedition, the cat will be out of the bag. How can you travel half-way around the world—presto?"

"Presto, just like that," said Hillory evenly. "Remember my last report on my psi project? You'll recall that...but let me talk to you in private, in my lab. Say tomorrow morning. What you see there may make up your mind whether Serendipity takes on this project or not."

Clyde's thoughts seemed to revolve and then remember something with a start. "All right, Hillory. Tomorrow at your lab."

"Meanwhile," said Hillory, taking the metal scroll out of the computer's scanner, "I'll keep this with me. The mind-entity seems to be after it, so if any further animations and attacks occur, they'll be aimed at me."

The others looked relieved. "Though it eases our worry," said Barton frankly, "you're sticking your neck out, old man."

Hillory smiled deprecatingly. "Not as much as you think. I'm not playing here. Remember my specialty is psi phenomena, and I think I can handle the situation." He did not want to say anything about using the metal foil as "bait" for a trap, in case the mind-entity could somehow read thoughts and be forewarned. In fact, he deliberately kept from thinking about it.

He gestured for Merry to follow him to his lab. "Are we going to set up—" Merry began, but Hillory shushed her warningly, then took two odd-looking helmets out of a closet, handing one to the girl. They were made of bands of silvery metal surmounted by a faceted crystal which began to glow softly.

"Now we can safely talk," said Hillory, but he did not move his lips. His thought-words went directly into Merry's brain and only to her.

"As you know," Hillory beamed at the girl, "these helmets create what might be called closed-circuit telepathy. I devised them only as a means of establishing mutual telepathy between two people. But they serve admirably now to keep our thoughts concealed from the mind-entity."

"You think he can read minds, if not sealed off?" said Merry in their weird non-vocal conversation.

Hillory nodded and pointed at the big chart on the wall. Besides the familiar electromagnetic spectrum, it showed a new and strange series of "octaves" labeled the *Psi Spectrum*. Hillory's *avant-garde* researches into this paranormal realm had revealed a whole new roster of ESP abilities hidden within the human mind. The conscious and subconscious minds known to conventional psychology were only the tip of the iceberg whose hidden bulk concealed vast mental powers that could be tapped by scientific means.

He had in one stroke vindicated all the psychic phenomena formerly held suspect. He had proved that at rare times the human psyche could dip into that supernormal pool in various ways, accounting for all the tales of telepathy, clairvoyance, precognition, psychokinesis, and the rest.

But Hillory's great step ahead had been to bring the psi-powers within range of scientific instrumentation and to command them at will instead of by sheer accident. Yet oddly enough, he did not actually know how psi phenomena really worked. He was like Faraday using electricity to run an electric motor without knowing what electricity was at the time.

Hillory knew what the psi "spectrum" was *not*. It was not an ascending series of different wavelengths of energy waves. There were no detectable "waves" connected with psionics, no "beams", no "photons" that could be projected from one point to another. Just how a telepathic thought could reach from one mind to another, Hillory did not know. However, he did know that the tektite crystals on top of their helmets, carefully faceted in a complex pattern, could somehow allow their thoughts to flow back and forth.

Hillory pointed at the top division of his psi-chart, labeled *free mind*. "That's what our enemy is," he informed Merry. "And this means he can control or utilize all the other psi-powers. He uses psychokinesis, of course, to animate objects. Fortunately, it probably takes a tremendous amount of PK power each time, so that in between he must 'rest' and 'recharge' his psi-batteries, so to speak. He must draw that power from the psi 'pool' that pervades the whole universe, as I've detected." Hillory held up the metal scroll. "To trap the mind-entity, this will be the bait."

"But what kind of trap," queried Merry, "can possibly hold a free mind that can ooze through solid matter? No box nor cage could hold him."

"An electro-psi cage will," returned Hillory mysteriously. Without explaining further, he took a large copper-mesh net from a supply closet and fastened an electrical cable in the middle. Flinging the other end of the cable over a rafter above, Hillory pulled and the metal net was drawn to the ceiling. Hillory coiled up the other end of the cable for slack, then connected it to a power switchboard. Then directly underneath the hanging net he carefully placed the metal-foil scroll on a wooden box and beside it another psi-crystal.

"There," said Hillory. "The idea is that when the mind-entity comes for the metal map—in whatever animated form he has chosen—I'll drop the net over him while you turn on the power to 50,000 volts. The presence of the psi-crystal will act as a trigger to create an electropsychic 'cage' around him of great power—enough to 'electrocute' him in psi terms."

Merry nodded. "I remember how you put a white rat in a wire cage, along with a psi-crystal, and the white rat's brain literally exploded."

"But it wasn't the high voltage that killed him," added Hillory. "It was a strange kind of electro-psi energy, a weird combination of electrical and mental power. Those are poor terms to use, but there is no vocabulary yet for those psi phenomena."

"Will the mind-entity be killed in that trap?"

"No, I don't think so if he stays within the space enclosed by the net. Being a free mind with no encumbering brain matter around it, no psi 'explosion' will occur. But he will undoubtedly perceive that if he *touches* the netting, he'll get a terrific electro-psi 'shock' and be electrocuted. That will make him our prisoner. Then I'll hook up to him telepathically and hear his story. We want to know who or what he is, why he's after the metal map, and what the so-called treasure is. After that, we'll decide what his fate should be—whether or not he's too dangerous to exist"

"You can deliberately kill him?" asked Merry. "How?"

"Simply by lowering the net so its folds touch the floor—and the mind-entity. Then, poof, as an untold number of electro-psi 'volts' burn out his mentality."

The girl shuddered a little at the gruesome picture.

Hillory stared at her grimly. "This is no game of patty-cake. The mind-entity is perfectly ready to kill. The name of the game is… superdanger."

Merry forced a smile to her lips. "Okay, I won't go woman on you. The trap is set. What do we do now?"

"We'll pretend to be photographing the metal map, while it lies on the box. If we just left the lab, with the metal-foil unguarded, the mind-entity might be suspicious. As it is, even if he has been trying, he's been unable to read our minds, so he doesn't have the faintest idea we set up the trap. If he could somehow observe or see what we were doing, it would probably mean nothing to him. He's an alien mentality from another world and earthly things or their uses would be obscure to him." He grinned. "Or else I'm a damn fool optimist, and the trap will fail."

"Let's hope not," said Merry. "With that invisible menace striking Serendipity Labs, everyone is getting unnerved. I almost wish…" She stopped.

"We hadn't found the metal scroll?" finished Hillory. For a moment he was haunted too. The quiet air of scientific research at Serendipity Labs had been disturbed by the mind-alien's blood-chilling invisible threat. And they did not need the "excitement" that came with this. Science research into the unknown was exciting in itself, to the nth degree.

Hillory felt all this and yet felt too the stirring challenge of what had been unfolded by the metal scroll—the search for an unknown and unearthly "treasure", perhaps of immense scope. He wondered how to convey this to the girl, but she responded herself.

"I was being silly. What we may discover in terms of an extraterrestrial civilization far outweighs the danger involved." Her brown eyes flashed, and she thumbed her nose at an undefined enemy.

Hillory chuckled, then spoke seriously. "We'll continue to wear our ESP helmets to keep any telepathic leakage from warning Mr. Mind. But at the same time, I'm going to turn on my ESP-scope."

"The one that acts like a radarscope and detects any mentality approaching?"

Hillory nodded and flipped the switch of an electronic box with a small screen on top which began to show a regular pattern of squiggles.

"When a 'blip' forms among those squiggles, we'll know that another mind is creeping close," whispered Hillory. "How long we'll have to wait, I don't know. Seems the mind-alien should be satisfied we're alone and attack soon."

They began their ritual of seemingly taking pictures of the metal scroll. Hillory handled the camera and took various shots, stretching the process out to consume time. When he felt himself drooping, going into his second night without sleep, he took a pep pill. They were a staple item in Serendipity Labs where the times and tides of research waited for no man and often kept them up around the clock.

Suddenly the ESP-scope reacted, its rhythmic squiggles broken up by a fuzzy blob that grew in the center and expanded.

CHAPTER 6

"Hsst," said Hillory to the girl. She glanced fearfully at the door. In what animated guise would the mind-alien enter? The door opened and a tall figure came in. Merry gave a little shriek.

"Dr. Clyde…you?" Hillory gasped, almost as startled as if their enemy had arrived.

The director stared at them solicitously. "Saw your light on under the door and just wanted to be sure you two were all right." It was Clyde's habit to wander down the halls at night and check in on whoever might be working late.

"Just taking routine pictures of the metal scroll," said Hillory, with a warning glance at Merry. They could not reveal their mind-trap without risking the mind-alien reading Clyde's mind and being tipped off. Though Clyde seemed rather puzzled at the strange way they were going about their photography, he finally shrugged and left with a wave.

"What a let-down that was," said Hillory, half annoyed. "Well, next time…."

The clock-hand did not creep much further before Hillory again pointed silently at the ESP-scope. Again a fuzzy blip grew there. Hillory tensed and glued his eyes on the door. Although the ESP-scope was non-directional, he expected intrusion by the normal means.

"The window!" screeched Merry suddenly.

And with a crash of glass, a large hawk came flying in. Though the blow might have knocked out a normal bird, this hawk appeared to be unharmed, its beady eyes glittering strangely.

Hillory's mind whirled. The mind-alien had deliberately wafted himself up into the air to inhabit this flying creature for a sudden and unexpected attack through a window.

Without pause, the hawk swooped to the center of the lab and seized the metal scroll in its beak, ready to fly away with it. It was a ruse that might well have succeeded except for Hillory's plan.

Hillory broke from a shocked trance and shoved Merry toward the power switches, as he himself began lowering the copper net. As Merry knifed the switch, the lowering net billowed around the hawk. The bird blundered into the netting and there was a flash, followed by the repulsive odor of burning feathers and scorched flesh.

The next moment, the charred body of the hawk lay on the floor, its beak still holding the metal scroll.

"The mind-alien won't escape in the body he borrowed," panted Hillory triumphantly. "Nor will his free mind."

Hillory had lowered the net until its bottom folded upon itself over the floor, forming a misshapen bulging "cage". In the center of it, invisible, must be the captured mind-alien.

Hillory had to be sure. He swept off his ESP helmet, no longer needing it for secrecy, and spoke aloud. The words might not be heard as such, but the thoughts behind them would reach the alien.

"You, in the net! Speak up. You're caught in an electro-psi field, if you can understand. Your naked mentality touching the net will bring you oblivion. So, speak. You have no choice."

The clock ticked loudly in a deep silence that followed. Hillory glanced at Merry's uncertain face. Had they failed after all to trap their enemy?

But then there came a subtle hissing sound like a radio transmitter being turned on and sending out its carrier-wave. Hillory could feel the impact of that pre-ESP emanation on his brain. It was a powerful force—frighteningly powerful.

A moment later, the unspoken but perfectly clear thought-words came. "Quite clever, earthling, this trap. I underestimated you. I did not think your kind"—he said it as if speaking of lowly worms—"capable of such psi refinements."

"You can skip the lordly attitude," snapped back Hillory. "Now, just who are you? And I might remind you that if you don't care to answer my questions, I'll just drop the net lower so that it collapses on itself and leaves no space for you...."

"No need for childish threats," a thought came back scornfully, yet a bit fearfully. "Why should I not answer you? I am *Jorzz*!"

The name had been given pompously, flourishingly.

"Jorzz," said Hillory mildly. "So I'm Hillory and the girl is Merry. But tell me, were you always a free mind, born that way somehow?"

"No, I had a body once."

"What kind of body?"

"A human body."

"What world did you live on?"

"Kaljj, it was called, far from here. At the other end of this galaxy."

"What were you on your world?" pried Hillory, realizing the alien was not going to volunteer any more information than he had to.

"I was...." A hesitation, then with another mental flourish. "I was the Star King, ruler of a great world civilized for a million of your years."

Hillory winced. They were dealing with a mind of vast advancement. "You *were* the Star King you say. What happened to you?"

Reluctance was plain as the slow answer came, "I was deposed."

"Because you were a hated ruler?" bored in Hillory, slowly shaping up a picture of this one-time bodied mind.

"No," spat back Jorzz vehemently. "My people all swore by me and would follow me anywhere."

"Follow you where?" said Hillory shrewdly. "To conquer other worlds? And those other worlds defeated your warlike people and then deposed you? Is that the story?"

"Yes, if you must know," Jorzz came back bitterly.

How little "human nature" changed, marveled Hillory. Whether on earth or on a planet inestimably further ahead on the scale of higher civilization. Always there would be born those souls who schemed and plotted to gain power. And Hillory could vaguely sense how earth rulers and leaders lusted for power, that rule of many worlds would be a proportionately greater drive to an ambitious mind.

"But how did you become a free mind, separated from your physical body?"

"By a process you would not understand," said Jorzz witheringly.

Hillory had no comeback. It was true that he had been striving for some time to perfect a mind-separation device, without success.

"Is your body still alive?"

"Yes…and no," he said enigmatically.

"What does that mean?"

"It is unimportant."

There was a finality in the way the alien-mind said it that Hillory sensed and wondered about. But he changed the subject.

"As a free mind, you are able to animate objects via PK. And you did animate the skeleton from the flying saucer…my motorcycle… and the android?"

"Of course."

"Now comes the big jackpot question." Hillory took a breath. "Just why are you after the metal scroll?"

"To gather what has been hidden here on your world, by what you would call space pirates," came back frankly.

"You mean they buried some sort of 'treasure' here, as we guessed? What is that treasure?"

"It is nothing you could want or use, earthling, I assure you…."

"We'll be the judge of that," snapped Hillory. "What happened to the pirates, just for the record?"

"They were hounded by galactic lawmen and killed. Only one member of the band escaped, with the metal treasure map. But he died on earth in a crash."

"The skeleton in the flying saucer." Hillory glanced at Merry. "Well, that clears up that part of the story." To the mind-alien he said, in sudden astonishment, "But the map was made about 35,000 earth years ago. That was how long ago the pirates buried their treasure, and the last survivor died. That means you have existed for…35,000 years!"

"Naturally. As pure mind essence, I am immune to ordinary death. Through that time I wafted myself throughout the galaxy, always seeking a clue to the treasure. I stumbled on it, here on your obscure planet, at the same time you did—at the flying saucer wreck."

Hillory's head swam a little, at the thought of a disembodied mind flitting like a ghost from world to world, star to star, searching a whole galaxy of 200 billion suns and uncounted billions of planets. A search for a needle in a cosmic haystack.

"How did you keep from going mad?" Hillory could not help murmuring. "An endless search all that time, for 35,000 years…"

"Time? What is time? It has no real meaning for a free mind. Time is the rate of decay of living bodies, or the coming of old age, or the breakdown of metabolism. That is what it means to most living people. But in my body-free state, it is as though I began my search yesterday."

Hillory shook his head. He had to get away from confusing metaphysical concepts and get to the meat of the matter. "You have been trying to wrest the metal map away from us. That means you don't know its contents."

A silence followed that seemed to mean consent.

Hillory was puzzled. "But you are obviously able to pick up people's thoughts when they talk, as you're doing with me. Then, when you heard the first spot was Mount Everest, why could you not rush there and beat us to it? You could animate something to pick up whatever treasure is there. Why didn't you go?"

"For reasons of my own," said the entity mockingly.

"He's bluffing," interposed Merry Vedec suddenly. "The reason is because he doesn't know *where* Mount Everest is."

"Is that right, Jorzz?" demanded Hillory.

Again no answer, which indicated to Hillory that they had scored another point in this mental duel.

"Good thinking, Merry," said Hillory, not caring if Jorzz overheard. "It's really quite simple. Earth is a strange new world to Jorzz. He hasn't the slightest idea where Mount Everest is or any other place on earth."

He turned toward the net-cage and the invisible entity. "Then what good would the map do you if you had gained possession of it?"

"That is my worry, earthling."

Hillory made another leap in deduction. "I suppose you would have hidden it somewhere, then wafted to some world and recruited aliens to come to earth and pick up whatever lies at the four spots. Anything like that." He shrugged. "That's all academic now. You'll never get hold of the map now that you're trapped."

"Do you intend to kill me?" asked Jorzz in deadly calm.

"Well, I..." Hillory paused. He hadn't thought that far yet. Now it faced him. Should he lower the net and end the existence of this eerie free mind? Jorzz had tried to kill them and had nearly succeeded with Barton. Why have any scruples about killing him in turn?

Still, free mind or not, Jorzz had once been a human being, or so he claimed. Killing another human being in cold blood was murder, no matter how you looked at it. Furthermore, Jorzz might not be a threat to earth itself. Whatever the "treasure" was, it had been planted on earth accidentally, much as old-time maritime pirates would choose a lonely island that they never intended to live on.

And how could he be sure Jorzz was evil? Maybe Jorzz had a right to the treasure and….

Hillory suddenly started, as if snapping out of a spell. He now felt the psychic force probing within his brain—*hypnotism*, Jorzz had been subtly working on his mind to make Hillory release him.

"No," gritted Hillory aloud, trying to resist the impulse. "You're evil…I know it…I feel it I must lower the net…"

But Hillory's hands froze. His muscles turned to water. The hypnotic forces from the alien's powerful mind became a torrent. Along with it now came thought-words in a mesmeric chant "You…will…release…me…earthling.   You…cannot…resist…my…superior…mental…forces. *Release me*."

"No," panted Hillory, sweating and straining to keep the insidious voice out of his brain. A glance to the side showed that Merry was in a trance, having gone under already and powerless to help.

"RELEASE ME!" came thunderously over the ESP channels.

Agonized, Hillory saw his hands begin to pull on the cable, slowly, unwillingly. The copper netting began to rise, inch by inch.

"No…no," choked Hillory, some part of his mind still resisting. But now most of his brain was overtaken by the tidal wave of hypnotic power that surged from the mind-alien. Muscles obeying the silent commands, Hillory mechanically pulled on the cable until the copper mesh cleared the floor.

Then suddenly the hypnotic force released him. Hillory let go of the cable and the net dropped to the floor—but too late.

"I'm free!" exulted Jorzz. "I wafted out from under the net. And now, idiot earthling…"

A heavy chair was suddenly animated and flung itself at Hillory. He barely ducked in time, as reflexes went into action. A ghostly psychic laugh sounded from thin air. "I'm leaving now. You still have the metal map. But the treasure will be mine…mine."

A last burst of mockery and then silence.

CHAPTER 7

Free of their spells, Hillory and Merry looked at one another dizzily, almost staggering on their feet. They felt as if they had battled a raging wind. Struggle in the psychic realm was more exhausting than physical battle.

"We failed," said Hillory hollowly, motioning for Merry to turn off the power in the cable. Then he picked up the metal map and stared at it. "This is going to be the toughest treasure hunt in history. Wherever we go, Jorzz can follow us like a shadow. Harass us. Maybe kill us."

"Are you thinking of giving it all up?" Merry ventured.

"Yes. I'll leave it up to chance."

"The toss of a coin?"

"No. But if the sun doesn't rise tomorrow morning, I'll give up the treasure hunt."

There was a half-humorous glint in Hillory's eyes now, plus a flash of steely resolve. He was himself again. "So Jorzz won this round. Well see who wins the bout when it's all over."

He turned to the girl. "But of course," he said with serious concern, "it's too dangerous for you to go along with me…"

"I'll scratch your eyes out if you say another word." Merry stood with eyes flashing, her small fists clenched. "I've been in this from the start, and I demand equal rights in seeing it through."

"Be sensible, Merry. A woman…"

"Leave out the chivalry rot."

"We might have to carry weapons."

"I'm the women's pistol champ in this state."

"You'll be risking your life."

"Who has the better right?"

"Merry, for your own sake…"

"Good. It's settled then. I go."

Hillory opened his mouth, shut it, and threw up his hands in surrender. He stared at the girl, wonderingly, as if seeing her for the first time.

"It's simple," explained Merry. "I joined the staff of Serendipity Labs for excitement. Sure, it was excitement of the more intellectual kind. But I was hoping for—serendipity. The big chance. And it came. The biggest and greatest adventure I could dream of." Her eyes glowed.

"And all that packed into 109 pounds," marveled Hillory. "But the big hurdle is to convince Dr. Clyde that we should carry out this hunt ourselves. Tomorrow morning I have to give him the clincher, in the form of a psi demonstration."

He yawned, his craving for sleep at last overcoming him. He put the metal scroll under the copper net, signaled Merry to turn on the power, and lowered the cable. "Safe for the night."

* * * *

Wearing the helmet surmounted by the faceted crystal, Hillory became hazy as a shimmering bubble seemed to form around him. He drifted gently off the floor up to the ceiling.

Dr. Clyde stared, along with Merry Vedec and Jim Barton, all gathered in Hillory's psi-lab. "I saw that demonstration last year," said Clyde, waving a lax hand.

"That won't convince me to send you on the treasure hunt."

"But it will in a minute," said Hillory, coming down lightly to stand in front of Clyde. "I've been perfecting this method of…well, call it psi-levitation. It's really a form of PK, or psychokinesis. That is, my mind's PK forces can be beefed up by the psi crystal to move my body at any rate of speed I want and to any distance. And I'll prove it."

The shimmering bubble with Hillory in it moved to the window, which had been left open. Hillory's face showed frowning concentration and then suddenly the bubble shot into the air at fantastic speed. The next moment it was gone.

"Wh-where did he go?" gasped Clyde.

"You'll find out in a moment," said Merry mysteriously. Barton spoke up. "Tell me more about that mind-trap you tried last night, Merry."

The girl gave a digest of the event. Five minutes later the phone rang. "Answer it, Dr. Clyde," said Merry, handing him the receiver.

"Long distance for Dr. Ames Clyde, from London."

"I'm Dr. Clyde."

"Here's your party, sir."

"Hello, chief. Hillory calling."

"From London?" gulped Clyde unbelievingly. "3,500 miles away?"

"Oh, I knew I loafed a bit on the way," said the phone. "But if I really hurry…"

The telephone cut off.

"…I can return before you hang up the phone."

It was Hillory's own voice as his bubble drifted into the window. Clyde sat there stunned, still holding the phone. He finally put it down with a sheepish grin.

"All right, Hillory. You've proved your psi-levitation can whisk you anywhere on earth, I suppose, in a second."

"No, chief. Instantaneously, if I wish."

Clyde glared indignantly. "Come, man. That would be faster than light."

"Exactly," nodded Hillory. "Psi phenomena are not limited by the laws of physical science."

"But how does it work? What are psi forces? Are they like electromagnetic radiations…radio waves…space-piercing pulsations… what?"

"None of those, chief." Hillory's craggy face took on a vague look. "To tell you the truth, I haven't the foggiest notion how it works. It can't be any kind of radiation because that has to be propagated, in quantum bundles of energy, across space itself with final velocity the classic 'c' of Einstein. Psi force is far faster than that, close to infinite speed. If I could concentrate the great amount of PK force needed, I could whisk across the whole universe as fast as I came from London back here."

"But how…how…does it work?" pleaded Clyde.

"The closest analogy I can give you," said Hillory slowly, "is hydraulics. When a pipe is filled with water and you put pressure at one end with a piston, that pressure is immediately felt at the other end. No, not immediately. Transmission time is measurable. But now think of a sort of *mental ether* that I think pervades the entire universe. It fills all the spaces between molecules, atoms, electrons, protons, and the rest. It exists in the so-called empty space between stars and galaxies too."

"Mental ether," muttered Clyde. "Fantastic."

"Maybe so. But think of this psi-ether as being completely non-compressible. Now, like in our water pipe, any psi 'pressure' or force you apply at one spot can be *instantly* felt at whatever other spot you've chosen as target. Do you see how this eliminates all need for wave-motion and radiation?"

"But how can the pressure speed all the way there so rapidly?"

"You're not following me," said Hillory patiently. "The psi-pressure doesn't have to 'speed' or travel anywhere. The pressure at one spot is transmitted through the non-compressible medium simply because of its all-pervading presence. It's like a man stepping on the brakes in his car and the hydraulic pressure manifests itself at the brake drums almost instantly. However, it wouldn't work on a car a mile long. The hydraulic pressure would take too long to be manifested at the braking end because all fluids are slightly compressible. The key is that the psi-ether is absolutely non-compressible. Hence it transmits psi-pressure in a timeless moment. No time passes at all."

"Sometimes I hate myself for asking questions," sighed Clyde wearily. He made a gesture as if to clear away cobwebs. "Forget the theory. I see that your psi-levitation works. If you can reach Mount Everest, and the other treasure spots, in the wink of an eye, you will obviously finish the job faster than any government agency. I will take it upon myself, under those circumstances, to keep this as an in-house project of Serendipity Labs."

Worry nagged the director somewhat, but not too much. They never worked on security projects for the government, pursuing their own independent researches. Their funding had originally come from a foundation and was now fattened by their by-product discoveries of commercial value. As long as the treasure hunt project represented no threat to earth itself—and nothing so far indicated such a threat—Clyde felt free in his conscience to make his decision.

By serendipity, a great plum had fallen into the lap of Serendipity Labs. Clyde was human enough to want all the glory to come to his establishment, once the mystery from the stars was cleared up.

"But you can't go alone, Hillory," admonished Clyde, assuming his role as director. "I won't allow it. Too dangerous, with that mind-alien dogging your footsteps, no doubt. Can your psi-levitation system transport more than one person?"

"Three," said Hillory. "I can crank up enough PK power from my mind, through practice, to expand the levitation bubble to hold three persons and all their gear—heavy clothing, food, water, weapons, whatever is needed."

"Who is to go along with you? Any choices?"

"Merry Vedec for one."

At the director's instant negative reaction, the flashing-eyed girl had to go through the whole argument she had with Hillory.

"What is this?" she finished passionately in what was not oratory but honest indignation. "Medieval times? The Victorian Age? Don't you gentlemen know women won the vote long ago? Total indiscrimination of federal jobs? And equal rights before all courts? There've been women hunters, explorers, gold miners. Will you kindly leave sex out of this and just consider me member number two of this expedition to Mount Everest. Thank you. *That's* settled."

Looking like a steamroller had run over him, Clyde switched and said, "Number three?"

"Barton," said Hillory. "I spoke with him before, and he's set to go."

"Eager is the word," put in Barton firmly. "Since Brains was used in breaking down the alien map's code, I feel personally involved. Me, I'm ready."

"But you haven't solved where the other treasure spots are yet," persisted Clyde. "Shouldn't you and Brains be working on that while Hillory is gone?"

"No use," said Barton. "Brains is completely stumped over the other spots. He can't solve them until he gets the right map of earth 35,000 years ago. The map we used happened to be right only for Mount Everest to be located. But other spots around earth will take better maps. I sent out a call, through the Research Data Center, for any and all theoretical maps of ancient earth of that time. It'll take some time before they're hunted down, xeroxed, and sent to us. So I'm free to go with Hillory."

"What about all the other problems that come up with our science researches here? You're the only one who can program Brains to solve them."

"Not any more," denied Barton. "I got an idea and asked Brains if he could be rigged to take vocal instructions and program himself. He came through with the right twist in the circuit. Any of the boys can just pick up the mike and read off his problem to Brains."

Clyde smiled a bit maliciously. "Sounds like you've just jockeyed yourself out of a job."

Barton grinned. "Don't worry. Brains is going to ask them to 'rephrase' their questions and 'modify' their equations and 'clarify' their points, over and over, until they get dizzy. They'll be glad when I come back and do it all for them. Brains and I talk the same language."

"Then it's settled that Merry and Jim Barton will go with me to Mount Everest," said Hillory, his mind rapidly making plans. "Now we come to equipment. We'll need blizzard suits and oxygen masks and all other things mountain climbers use, in case we have to search the tip of Mount Everest. Secondly, we'll take along a week's supply of food and water, just in case. Thirdly—weapons."

Barton glanced at him sharply. "Not against any wild beasts, which don't exist on Mount Everest's tip, but against Mr. Mind."

"Or rather, whatever forms he animates," amended Hillory. "Ordinary guns might not be effective against, say, a moving rock. We need something more powerful."

"A laser gun," said Clyde instantly. "Dr. Peabody has such a device which came out of his power-ray researches. I'll see that you get one to take along. Hmm, to round up all the things you need will take a couple days...."

"Make it 24 hours, chief," interposed Hillory urgently. "The less time we waste the better, giving the mind-alien less chance to operate against us."

"Browbeater," sighed Clyde accusingly. "Twenty-four hours it is."

CHAPTER 8

All the staff of Serendipity Labs watched from the roof as the queer bubble wafted into the air with its three passengers.

Hillory shifted his weight on the pile of supplies on which they sat. "Ready?" he said to Jim Barton and Merry Vedec. Both were somewhat tense now that the actual moment had arrived. The thought of being weirdly transported halfway around the world by pure mental forces was not restful on the nerves. But they both nodded firmly.

Hillory's rugged face took on an expression of concentration. His forehead furrowed as he built up psi power through the faceted crystal on his helmet. By some para-psi process that Hillory understood only vaguely, the tektite crystal was able to tap the vast universal pool of "mental ether" that existed all around limitlessly.

As if he were a human receptacle, this psi-power flowed into his brain. When he felt as if his mind would burst, he gave the mental command for the bubble to move. Converted into PK energy, the psi-power whisked the bubble away. It vanished from the view of the watchers below.

"I couldn't make it an instantaneous flight," gasped Hillory, easing back a little now that they had started. "Too much load."

"But we'll get there faster than any jet plane," observed Merry, looking down at the blurred landscape below.

Barton tentatively poked out a finger to touch the side of the bubble. It felt rubbery and gave a little. "Just what is it made of?"

Hillory shrugged. "Call it psi-plastic. It comes from my practice in using psi-transmutation, or the creation of mental material, living or nonliving."

"Sort of like firm ectoplasm," put in Merry with an impish smile. "Ghost-stuff made tough."

Hillory nodded a bit wryly. The ectoplasm that spiritualists claimed to produce had always been scoffed at by orthodox science. Hillory did not scoff. He also produced and used the stuff. All his psi-feats were of this eerie nature at the borderland between material science and psychic manifestations.

Yet the ectoplasmic bubble was real and remarkably tough, once formed. It protected them from all the howling wind resistance as it propelled them through the air at about mach 20.

"But just how," persisted Barton, "can you make something material out of pure mental forces?"

Hillory sought for words. "In orthodox science, matter can be turned into energy and vice versa. In psi-science, the psi-ether or 'energy' can also be turned into psi-matter. Result, this bubble. It's as simple as that."

"Simple," snorted Barton, giving his handlebar mustache a twist. "And all you use to pull these psi-tricks is that small crystal on your helmet? How and why does that work?"

Below, they were rushing over the Atlantic Ocean and coming up to the shoreline of northern Africa. Hillory had "set a course" in that direction, toward the Himalayas. There was time yet to talk.

"My psi-crystal is made of tektite, a very mysterious substance. Scientists have never been agreed whether they are bits of volcanic glass formed here on earth or splashings of meteoric impacts on the moon that were hurled into space and reached earth. It so happens they're both wrong."

Someday, Hillory would announce all this to the world. But it was still too soon. Orthodox science still stood as a solid block against all paranormal and psi phenomena as being "kook" concepts. Hillory knew that a paper on tektites, giving their true origin, could never be presented before any contemporary scientific society.

"Tektites," Hillory explained for Barton, "are crystallizations of the psi-ether. How or why it happens I don't know. I only know that they are psi-energy turned into matter. As such, they act like 'transistors' for the flow of psi-power. They form a link between my mind—or anybody's mind—and the all-pervading psi-ether pool of power. And that power is immense. I've only drawn off tiny amounts of it at times. So, in summary, the tektites are the trigger or valve or 'switch' that allow me to pull down psi-power and channel it in whatever way I need it."

Hillory stopped and switched to more practical matters.

"We're getting close to Mount Everest. Start putting on those parkas. When we step out of the bubble, we'll be going from comfortable conditions into a bitter below zero climate with howling winds and maybe a blizzard."

They took turns dressing in the cramped interior of the bubble. Soon all were clad in the furred jumpers that covered all but face and hands. Heavy gloves were also ready, and oxygen masks.

They peered down excitedly as the mighty ramparts of the snow-capped Himalaya mountains shouldered hugely over the horizon. Standing out majestically from the towering horde was aloof Mount Everest. Unerringly, guided by mental commands from Hillory, the bubble slowed and gently touched down on a barren patch of rock at the tip. All else was wind-whipped snow and tumbled ice.

Hillory pointed his finger at the bubble's side, outlining a round circle. Then, at the mental command, the material vanished to leave an open door. Instantly, a gust of frigid air came in that made them all gasp.

They adjusted their oxygen masks, already feeling the lung-heaving thinness of air six miles high. Hillory lumbered out first, leaning into the wind and gesturing for the other two to follow. They looked around, hardly able to see more than ten yards in the swirls of snow that constantly eddied around in the fierce wind.

Just what they were searching for they didn't know. They had gone through it all before. Their only plan was to hike around and look for anything unusual—a rock hollow, a cave, anything that might be a cache for a "treasure".

The actual tip of Mount Everest, the highest point, was not a large area, just a few acres of flat rock and icy snow. On all sides were sheer drops or treacherous ridges of slanting ice. An occasional glimpse through the dancing snowflakes gave a giddy, soul-squeezing view down for long miles to the sea level valleys.

Methodically, Hillory began tramping around the outer perimeter of the flat mountain tip and gradually spiraled inward. They saw nothing that could even remotely be considered a hiding place secure from the elements and the ravages of time.

Where would the space pirates of long ago have hidden their unknown "loot" so as to be safe for centuries? Their search was blind.

"Serendipity," screeched Merry in the teeth of the wind. "It'll take that to find it."

And serendipity, Hillory reflected, was something you couldn't order forth or make come about. By definition it would have to be stumbling on it in the most unexpected place.

Unexpected... Hillory mused on that. What if the hiding place were not anywhere in the rock and ice around them but somewhere else? Yet where would that be? He pondered the paradox, baffled.

Before long they came upon the small stone shrine that had been constructed at the spot where the first conqueror of the world's tallest peak had planted the flag. It was in honor of Sir Hillary—and for the first time, Hillory realized it was almost his namesake. A quirk of fate.

But all else at the mighty mountain's tip was bare. There was not even a rock niche in sight where a box or container might be stashed in reasonable safety for a length of time.

The unexpected would be...it suddenly flashed on Hillory...u*p*. Not on the tip but off. Barton and the girl stared wonderingly as they saw Hillory brace himself against the wind and gape upward.

"No planes or eagles or anything fly up here," shouted Barton. "What do you see, Hillory?"

"Nothing...yet. Wait...."

Hillory wiped his tearing eyes with the back of his furred glove and squinted upward again. Dimly through the eternal windblown snow chaff he saw something square. Something manmade and unbelievably hanging in mid-air a hundred feet up.

Thoughts lanced through Hillory's mind. "Up there," he pointed. "Mountain climbers would never look for it and thus never see it. Besides, the never-dying wind blowing snow around would always make it obscure. Yet it would be plainly visible to people coming in a powerful flying saucer."

"A box," screamed Merry, seeing it finally. "But how can it stay anchored there, in a hurricane-fast wind, for ages?"

"A gravity anchor," hazarded Hillory. "Some force beam or whatever holding it firmly in position, defying the worst winds."

"Well, we found it," yelled Barton, in triumph mixed with dismay. "But how do we get it down?"

Hillory was already fumbling in a large breast pocket to pull out one of his faceted tektite crystals. "I'll try PK power," he told them. He fastened his gaze on the glowing pseudo-gem as if it were a tiny crystal ball. From some great psi-reservoir psychic power flowed into his brain, then out from his mind and upward. An uncanny clutching force seized the floating box and tried to yank it down. But it did not move.

"They set up a very strong gravity anchor," said Hillory, sweating. "Got to pour in PK-power by the carload…."

The very air seemed strained as two fantastic forces—gravity and psi—battled each other. Hillory gasped with the effort he threw into it, and his face became drawn. The psi-tektite in his hand was glowing fiercely now, almost like a hot coal. It was like an electrical cable sucking in megawatts of power and coming close to a short circuit that heated the wires within.

Abruptly, an audible snap sounded in the air.

"It's moving," shrilled Merry, dancing in joy. "It's coming down."

The box drifted down now, under Hillory's mental control. "Broke the gravity-anchor," he crowed. "Psi-forces, in the end, are more powerful than any other known forces."

As the box bumped at their feet, Barton grabbed it up excitedly. It was made of metal that seemed uncorroded through the ages. But a thin patina of tarnish spoke of the tremendous length of time it had survived, some 35,000 years. No other details could be noticed on the box, not even the edge of a lid. It seemed like a sealed container.

Barton hoisted it to his shoulder with a grunt. "Come on. We'll open it in the bubble—if we can."

He started off, but Hillory grabbed his arm. After Hillory swung his face this way and that, he pointed. "The bubble's that way. Used some psi-radar, so to speak."

Barton shivered. "Lucky you've got those weirdo powers, or we could get lost in this patch of frozen hell forever."

Passing a rocky edge, Merry suddenly screamed. "That hand! Something's crawling up here."

The men whirled and saw the distorted shape that crawled over the edge and stomped toward them, looming hugely.

"A yeti," barked Hillory. "One of the legendary abominable snowmen—only he isn't a legend. And he's been animated—taken over mentally—by Mr. Mind, of course. Our enemy has struck."

Making queer guttural sounds in its throat, the hairy giant lumbered toward them, clawed hands outstretched. In panic, Barton tried to run but his foot slipped on a patch of ice. He sprawled on his face, the box sliding from his hands.

Hillory darted toward the box, but Merry screamed a warning. The misshapen manlike creature had raised a huge chunk of ice in its hands and was hurling it straight at Hillory. Hillory dodged frantically, but the edge of the ice caught him in the shoulder and spun him about. He lost his footing and fell heavily, his breath knocked out.

The grotesque monster-man now brushed Merry aside like a doll and stooped to pick up the heavy box like a toy. He began trotting away with it "The mind-alien…he's getting away with it," groaned Barton, standing groggily on his feet and lurching forward without hope of overtaking the yeti.

On his knees, clearing his dizzy senses, Hillory thought fast. He fumbled the tektite crystal out of his pocket and concentrated. Piling up psi-power, he released it in one shattering stab of PK force. If his aim was right….

Like the crack of doom, a tall pinnacle of ice broke off and thudded down squarely on the yeti's head. The creature's knees buckled, and it slowly crumpled into the snow. The metal box tumbled out of his limp hands.

"Hope that gave Mr. Mind a good headache," growled Hillory as he ran forward and picked up the box. The yeti itself lay dead with its skull crushed. But then, ghoulishly, it stirred…moved…staggered to its feet.

"Good God," cried Hillory, shaken. "But of course, since he could animate that dead alien skeleton at the flying saucer, he can animate that yeti, dead or alive."

The ghastly undead monster, with blood dripping down its lifeless face and closed eyes, began lurching after Hillory. It turned then, to cut him off from reaching the bubble. Hillory stooped as Barton and Merry came up.

"Can't reach the bubble," Hillory panted. "And I'm too drained of psi-power right now to use any psi-tricks on him."

As if aware that his quarry was trapped, the undead horror came stumbling toward them, hairy arms swinging as if to seize them and rip them apart. Barton broke from their horrified trance.

"This way…a place to hide…"

Following Barton, they came to a towering mound of ice with a crevice in front. It was just wide enough for the men to squeeze through, after Merry. Hillory managed to pull the box in with him. They stood in a cul-de-sac about six feet wide. Its only entrance was the crevice, too narrow for the giant monster-man to come through.

"But we're still trapped…cornered," Merry half-whimpered. "And it's trying to get at us."

CHAPTER 9

They could hear the yeti's powerful claw-hands ripping away at the ice crevice trying to widen it. Chunks of ice slowly began to fall away.

"He's got quite a job there," rasped Barton. "And I haven't had a chance to use this yet." He pulled out his laser-gun. "I'll shoot him and...."

Barton choked and his eyes turned wild. "My God, what am I saying? He's already dead." He composed himself with an effort "Still, it's worth a try."

He aimed the pistol-sized weapon through the crevice where the yeti's hairy body could be seen. As he pulled the trigger, a ruby beam spat forth viciously and burned through the creature's hide. The activities of the monster continued without a halt.

"Drilled a hole clear through him without effect," groaned Barton. Savagely, he shot again and again, raking the yeti from head to foot. No sound came from it, no cry of pain. How could a dead thing cry in pain? And what could stop its massive, muscled bulk from continuing to rip away at the ice crevice?

They all looked at each other, fear shining from their eyes.

"Gun's empty," Barton half-sobbed, flinging the weapon away. "If I had had enough shots, I could have riddled him with enough holes until he fell apart like rotten cheese. But he's still a working machine of dead flesh...."

The horror of it overwhelmed them. Merry ran her glove over the metal box. "Inside lies the first part of the unknown treasure, but we won't live to see it. So near and yet so far...."

They all felt the ironic agony of that, having gotten on the verge of some tremendous secret of the far past only to face doom.

"Psi-power," snapped Hillory. "Our only hope. I'm still too depleted to do it alone...but if both of you help...."

Hillory held his tektite crystal before their eyes. "Stare at it... concentrate your mind on it. You'll trigger off a flow of psi-energy from the psi-ether. You don't know how to utilize it, but I think I can manipulate it for our purposes."

Barton and the girl did as they were told. They began to feel something of the awesome power they were tapping as it torrented through their minds. Hillory sighed a brief prayer and then sent out a mental probe, seeking to link up with their psi-currents.

"Ah, got it," he breathed. "Now to form them into one single force, together with what I can muster on my own, and...."

Something akin to an explosion occurred beyond the ice crevice. They could see the yeti's dead body flying apart into bloody fragments that scattered for yards.

Barton stared in shock. "What in heaven's name was that?"

"Call it psi-dynamite," sighed Hillory. "That was the only thing to do. Mr. Mind can't put Humpty Dumpty back together again. We're free of the yeti menace."

Hillory looked around grinning. Somewhere the invisible mind-alien, after being blasted out of the body, must be hovering in chagrin, knowing he had lost.

"How was that, Jorzz?" Hillory chortled aloud. "Your Frankenstein bit flopped."

Something like a mental curse snapped out of nowhere. Then a raging thought-voice. "Gloat while you can, earthling. But your labors have been for nothing. You will see what I mean when you get the box open."

"What's inside?" said Barton. "We've got to find out. Is he fooling us or what?"

"It'll have to wait until we get back to the labs," said Hillory, as they trudged to the bubble. "It's a sealed container and will take a high-temp torch to melt it open." Inside the psi-bubble the icy winds were cut off to their relief. Their fingers were half-frozen and their faces frostbitten. Barton gave a short laugh as they sat on the pile of food supplies. "A week's worth, and we didn't stay half a day."

"We can always use them for further expeditions," observed Merry.

But what concerned them most was the strange metal box that had hung for 35,000 years in mid-air above Mount Everest. On the trip back home, Barton kept looking for a seam or crack to indicate a lid but found nothing. It was as tightly sealed as an eggshell.

What did it contain?

* * * *

At Serendipity Labs Dr. Clyde and others were present as a special high-temperature cutting torch was used to slice open the metal box. It offered no particular resistance. When it was cooled, Hillory stepped forward to lift off the severed portion.

Within lay a mass of pulpy material as if to insulate its contents from extremes of heat or cold. Hillory dug his hands into the stuff and felt something hard. He withdrew a globular object that sparkled with crystalline brightness, sending out shafts of all colors of the rainbow.

"A jewel?" gasped Merry. "Some kind of giant gem that is rare in the universe?"

"No, I don't think so," said Hillory, turning the queer ball in his hands and peering closely. "Wait…it's hollow inside."

Staring through the multi-colored flashings, he could see inside the hollow globe. What he saw brought a puzzled frown to his face. It seemed to be a thin flat strip of blackish material that was coiled up tightly, filling the interior space.

"Odd," he exclaimed. "It looks like a *tape* of all things."

"Tape?" echoed Barton.

"Yes, like that from a tape recorder or a video tape for television," returned Hillory baffled.

"And that's all?" said Merry, disappointed.

"Some 'treasure'," grunted Barton, giving his mustache a frustrated twist.

"Ah, but suppose," said Dr. Clyde, "that tape when played back shows their civilization on a far-off world. That would be a scientific 'treasure' indeed."

"But why would space pirates bother to steal it and carefully hide it?" said Hillory doubtfully. "It must be more than that. Well, no use speculating. Let's get it open and take the tape out—if it is a tape."

But there lay the rub. They couldn't get the rainbow-hued globe open. It went from lab to lab, subjected to high-powered drills, saws and chisels, then pyrogenic torches that could make stone run like water.

"Not a dent or scratch or mark on it," muttered Hillory. "What is it made of? We'll have to try the nutcracker."

The "nutcracker" was a giant press capable of squashing solid steel balls into flat pancakes. The machine groaned and creaked as power was applied to its peak load, but nothing happened. The crystal globe, looking as fragile as an eggshell, showed not the slightest effect.

Hillory tried the most drastic method, even at the risk of damaging the tape within. The globe was placed inside an armored steel drum in which a high explosive was set off. Even a diamond the size of a globe would have been shattered.

But when the lid had been removed and the smoke gushed out, Hillory looked down and held his head. "That didn't even knock off one molecule."

"Bring it in to Dr. Cheng," suggested Merry. "He's working toward the goal of what he calls indestructible matter."

In Lab No. 5, the dwarfish Oriental scientist turned the globe over in his hands wonderingly, as Hillory told the story of their attempts to open it.

"It must be matter with interlocked atoms," he breathed. "Let me try my ultra-laser which can drill through anything known."

"Known to our science," murmured Hillory, but too low for Dr. Cheng to hear.

The little scientist aimed a tubular device at the globe and tripped a switch. A tiny red spot appeared on the surface of the globe. It brightened as Dr. Cheng rammed more power through. His eyes widened as minutes went by and the red spot did not change. Hillory watched, fretting inwardly with a hopeless feeling.

An hour later, the little scientist snapped off his ultra-laser and peered at the globe with a magnifying glass. Then he sat at his desk, put his head down on his arms, and began sobbing.

"They achieved it! Someone else besides me found the secret of... *indestructible matter*."

"Are you sure?" said Hillory swallowing.

Dr. Cheng lifted his tear-wet eyes. "My equations show that atoms interlocked in a certain pattern are impervious to any outside force. Someone else in the universe knows the secret...and I don't."

Hillory and Merry left him sobbing brokenly. They could understand his emotional storm in a way. It was a shattering blow for Dr. Cheng to know that another mind had accomplished a feat that he had failed to perform after years of hard effort.

But to Hillory, it was a far worse dilemma. "What if the other three portions of the treasure are the same? Or something, anyway, encased in that impenetrable substance? Maddening!"

"I feel like screaming," admitted Merry.

Merry did scream a moment later as they passed Lab No. 8 with lettering on the door—DR. JONAS T. SPINDLE, BIOLOGIST. The door had abruptly swung open to frame a nightmarish sight. A huge quivering mass of amorphous flesh came squeezing through with a horrible squishing sound.

"Dr. Spindle's giant amoeboid," screeched the girl. "It escaped. Or else"—terror sprang into her eyes—"it's animated by Mr. Mind…."

Hillory had already come to that conclusion and yanked the girl back. But a rubbery pseudopod formed in the jellylike mass and whipped forth like a tentacle. Slimy coils began to wrap themselves around the two, dragging them toward the slurping creature.

A picture flashed through Hillory's mind of one-celled amoebas under a microscope, drawing in their prey and smothering it, absorbing it. Hillory shuddered, unable to break the grip of the tentacle as he and Merry were inexorably drawn closer to the loathsome superamoeba.

Others had come running at Merry's scream but stood helplessly. There was no way to tackle the huge shapeless hulk that spread from side to side and blocked the hallway. A greedy maw opened up in the amoeboid's flexible flesh, ready to gulp in its two victims.

But Hillory suddenly remembered the crystal globe in his hands and began to pound at the tentacle with it. The hard blows began to hammer the fleshiness into loose pulp until it snapped apart. As the tentacle went limp, Hillory flung it aside and dragged Merry free. "Inside the lab," he panted.

"But it's following us," whimpered Merry as the amorphous monster quickly oozed back through the doorway. It slurped hungrily as if aware that its victims were now trapped in the lab.

But there was purpose in Hillory's movements as he darted to the wall and unhooked a huge spray device. Using the pump-handle, he sprayed a greenish mist at the giant amoeba, which immediately began to shiver and shrink back.

Hillory kept spraying madly and gradually the massive amoeboid became quiescent and still, no longer quivering. It appeared dead.

"Dr. Spindle's anesthetizing spray," explained Hillory, hanging up the sprayer. "He developed it to keep his playmates under control. But what happened to him—?" Merry was already bending over the scientist's limp form, lying slumped in a corner. Dr. Spindle's eyes opened dazedly, then he sat up in alarm. "Jumbo, my giant amoeboid! It oozed out of its tank…knocked me aside with a pseudopod and…."

"Relax," said Hillory, pointing at the unmoving hulk. "It attacked us, but I gave it your bug spray."

"Thank heaven." But the scientist's eyes looked pained. "My amorphoids never menaced anyone before, with the precautions I took. I'm sorry, Hillory…."

"No need to apologize. It wasn't your fault. The mind-alien—you've heard about him—entered Jumbo and animated him into a killer."

"Oh," said Dr. Spindle in infinite relief.

Hillory eyed the gelatinous mound blocking the door. "The question now is, how do we get out?"

"Just climb over it," said Dr. Spindle. "Don't worry, you won't sink in."

Distastefully, Hillory and Merry clambered up over the hulk, hand in hand, finding it rubbery under their feet but otherwise quite firm. From the other side, Hillory called back.

"Just how will you get it back in its tank?"

"Leave that to me," came Dr. Spindle's voice. "I have a sort of giant suction pump that does the job."

"Jorzz just won't give up," said Merry, looking around with a shiver. "He's stalking us all the time."

"And this time he was after this globe," said Hillory worriedly, glancing at the adamant ball in his hand. "If he can't get the metal map from us, he'll try to seize each of the four treasures as we locate them. How can we keep them safe?"

"Keep them safe for what?" Merry said ironically. "If we can't even open them."

"We'll find a way sooner or later. Ah, I have an idea."

CHAPTER 10

DR. ENRICO TORREO, COSMOLOGY read the door of Lab No. 9.

A roly-poly man who at first glance seemed as wide as he was tall turned his flashing black eyes at Hillory and Merry.

"I'm glad you escaped from that amoeboid," he greeted them sincerely. "I watched in the hall. You look calm, but I'm still shaken." He held out his hands to show they were trembling.

"Maybe we're getting used to Mr. Mind's attacks," said Hillory, half-banteringly. Then he held up the crystal globe that constantly flashed rainbow hues from its polished surface. "As you've probably heard, this is the first 'treasure'—a strange globular container with tape inside."

"You never got it open?"

Hillory shook his head. "We have another problem. Where can we store this while we go out for the other three treasures? During our absence, Mr. Mind could strike and get hold of this globe. Is it possible to hide it...."

"Yes, in the fifth dimension," returned Torreo quickly and rather proudly. "And I'll guarantee that the mind-alien will never reach it there. What I'll do is project it...but here, let me demonstrate first."

"Fine," said Hillory in relief, having wanted to suggest that himself, before entrusting the treasure globe to an unknown process.

Torreo dramatically placed a book behind a plastic shield, inside of an oval-shaped device. "I won't attempt to explain precisely how it works, but I use a phased electrostatic probe that can project objects beyond our three dimensional world. Onionskin worlds, parallel worlds, call them what you will, but they exist within reach."

He pulled a switch, and the book vanished. "It hasn't moved," said Torreo. "Not an inch. Yet it's now far away in the fifth dimension, totally beyond reach. To bring it back...."

He reversed the switch. Though prepared, Hillory and Merry both jumped as the book sprang into view again.

"Seems closer to magic than science," said Merry.

'I've done this with hundreds of objects," said Torreo. "And always brought them back intact."

"I'm convinced," said Hillory, handing over the globe. Still, he felt misgivings as Torreo's device made it disappear.

Torreo noticed his expression and smiled. "Watch, I'll bring it back several times."

Three times the globe vanished, and twice it came back. The third time it purposely stayed in the fifth dimension. "That's that," sighed Hillory. "It's presumably safe from Mr. Mind—as safe as anything can be. Now we can go on with our treasure hunt."

"But the next thing," reminded Merry, "is to furnish Brains with a more authentic map of earth 35,000 years ago before we'll know where spot number 2 is."

* * * *

Barton took the map that Hillory held out. "Merry and I sorted through a couple dozen ancient maps of earth, according to the theories of various geologists. But we have no way of knowing which of them is nearest to being right. So we'll just have to try them out at random. This one first."

Barton nodded and fed the map to Brains, along with the alien scroll. He twiddled his mustache as he waited for the computer's preliminary scan. Then wording lighted up—EARTH MAP UNSUITABLE.

Barton grinned. "Wait'll the scientist who made that map of earth in 35,000 B.C. finds out that his pet theory is hogwash."

"Hmm," said Hillory. "A by-product of our project is that we can give the geologists a much more reliable map of prehistoric earth than they every had before. The aliens who buried the treasure gave us eyewitness data of that time with which to compare our guesswork maps."

Barton fed in five more maps which were summarily rejected by Brains. Hillory began to look worried. Would they all turn out wrong?

But the next map was accepted by the computer, which signaled with its lights that it needed 33 minutes and 7 seconds to locate spot number 2.

"Just time enough for a quickie lunch at the cafeteria," invited Hillory, taking Merry's arm. "Barton?"

"I've got to stay and catch up with in-house programmings to feed Brains, on the side." Barton went on nervously. "But what if our mental pal from outer space decides to grab the metal scroll while you're gone, with only me on guard? I don't like it."

"Neither do I," mused Hillory. He turned. "You go, Merry, and bring me back some sandwiches and coffee."

When the girl had gone, Hillory took out one of his psi-tektites and held it in his hand. "If the mind-alien comes anywhere near, I'll get a psi-warning. That will give me time enough to build up a psi-blast, ready to fire at anything dangerous."

"Good enough," said Barton, relaxing.

After Merry returned and Hillory ate absently, Brains was ready with his answer.

Barton pressed the voice read-out button and the sonorous tones of the computer came forth.

"The second spot of the alien map is on a continent that exists between South America and Africa...."

Barton punched the hold button and turned a stunned face. "Did you hear that?" he demanded. "That's the legendary continent of *Atlantis* out in the middle of the Atlantic Ocean."

"Obviously, it wasn't legendary," said Merry drily. "When the aliens came here 35,000 years ago, it was there—dry land where ocean liners cross today."

Hillory got over his shock and said, "It fits with the theories of sunken Atlantis, which was supposed to have submerged about 25,000 years ago. Various holocausts are given for this tremendous event, such as earth's axis shifting and what-not. And I remember now that the map Brains accepted did show a land mass in the Atlantic. It wasn't called Atlantis—cartographers are extremely sensitive about backing up 'myths'. But nevertheless, that map did hypothesize a continent that is now sunken."

He looked at the other two lugubriously. "Which brings up a unique problem. It means that we have to *dive* for our treasure this time."

"EEK is all I can say." Merry wasn't smiling. "But how far down?"

Hillory shrugged. "Brains wouldn't know that. He's dealing with the ancient world when Atlantis was up above. Well, let's hear what further data Brains can give."

Barton took the computer off hold, and the rest was revealed. "The treasure is located in almost the exact center of this continent, where there is a landmark consisting of a huge pit made by a giant meteorite that fell. The treasure is in the bottom of the pit."

"From the frying pan into the fire," commented Barton ruefully. "We not only have to go underwater, but reach the bottom of a pit." He turned to Hillory. "The question is, can your psi-bubble transport us under the sea?"

"That's a new one for me," admitted Hillory. "I only aimed at levitation through the air at comparatively low pressure. Diving down a mile or more will surround us with tremendous water pressure."

"If we have to ask Clyde for some sort of deep-sea diving vessel," said Barton glumly, "he'll probably refuse and turn the project over to the government."

Hillory jerked his body erect. "We can't let that happen. This project is our baby. But how in the world can we go down to a sunken world…."

He snapped his fingers. "Remember my psi-spectrum? Astral projection is the answer."

"What's that?" Barton asked warily.

"Well, it's sort of converting your physical body to a different plane of vibration and projecting it through matter without touching it."

"Like a ghost?" said Barton, aghast.

"Yes—and no. We don't separate our psyche from our body but turn our body into a psi-form, so to speak. In the psi or astral form, our bodies will then be impervious to water pressure when we descend into the ocean."

"Have you done this before?"

"Yes, but only to a limited degree, such as walking through a wall, or swimming underwater for a mile. To reach Atlantis, however, we'll have to stay in the astral state for hours."

Hillory turned to face the other two. "Look, I won't ask either of you to try this experiment. It could be dangerous. I'll go it alone…"

"The hell you will," said Merry.

"You took the words out of my mouth," added Barton. "Show me the ropes, and I'll ghost along with you down to Atlantis."

Hillory took them to his lab and spent the rest of the day showing them the technique. Merry and Barton each wore a helmet with a tektite crystal on top. Hillory instructed them in how to concentrate.

"It's really not hard. The tektite does the work and siphons down psi-power for you. You really *will* yourself to become astral."

Merry, who had shared much of Hillory's psi-experiments, caught on more quickly. Her body suddenly turned wraithlike, almost transparent. Barton stared, then concentrated, and also turned into a misty form.

"I can see right through you," said Merry impishly. She realized it was telepathy talk since her lips made no sound.

Experimentally, Barton poked his fist at the wall. He felt a weird cold feeling, but nothing solid was in his way.

"This is an oversimplification," said Hillory by way of explanation. "But all your atoms and molecules have speeded up their motions until you are at a totally different vibratory rate from ordinary matter. You can then 'ooze' through matter without being hindered."

"Say," said Barton suddenly. "Is that the form the mind-alien has?"

"No," said Hillory emphatically. "Don't get the different psi-states mixed up. Jorzz is a free-mind, something I haven't achieved yet. That means he has *separated* his mentality from his physical body and acts independently of it. In our case there is no such separation."

Barton swung his fist at the wall again, but this time there was a bruising thump and he jerked back with a howl of pain.

"You didn't hold your astral state long enough," grinned Hillory. "But now that you have the hang of it, you can practice staying in the astral state for more than an hour. And I have to practice right along with you."

A while later, the door opened and Dr. Clyde came in. He looked blankly at first, as if seeing nothing. Then he noticed the three ghost-like figures and turned white.

"Hillory...Barton...Merry Vedec. Are you dead?" he quavered.

Hillory snapped into view as a fully solid and real person. "Hardly, chief. Let me explain about where spot number two is on the alien map and what our method will be for finding the treasure."

When Hillory had finished, Clyde looked worried. "I don't know if I should let you try these paranormal experiments, risking your lives. Something might go wrong. The government could send down a deep-sea vessel...."

"And risk the lives of a big crew," put in Hillory. "Deep-sea stuff is no picnic, in any case. And I believe psi-powers can be more depended on than technology."

"Go to it then," sighed Clyde. "Do you need any special supplies?"

'That's the beauty of it," said Hillory. "In astral form we won't need deep-sea diving suits or air or anything. We can explore miles down in the ocean as if taking a stroll through a garden."

"How are you going to see down there?" said Clyde cannily. "It's pitch-dark in the ocean below 3,000 feet. And even if you find the treasure, how can your nonmaterial astral hands pick it up?"

Barton stared in shock at Hillory, as if suddenly aware of these problems. But Hillory was unshaken. "I've thought of all that, chief. And I have the psi-answers, I assure you."

Clyde threw up his hands and left wordlessly.

"We'll make our astral trip tomorrow," Hillory told his two companions.

CHAPTER 11

The psi-bubble again wafted itself away from Serendipity Labs, holding three passengers. It reached high-mach speed and swung over the Atlantic Ocean. Hillory consulted the earth map they had fed to Brains, showing the ancient landmass of Atlantis. He had marked down the latitude and longitude coordinates that the computer had supplied to the spot marked "X."

Barton used the Pathfinder, another Serendipity product which acted as a compass, sextant, and inertial guidance system all wrapped in one, leading them unerringly to a spot over the Atlantic that was their jumping-off point into the deep.

Hillory brought the bubble to a mid-air halt, just above the rolling waves. He pointed straight down. Then he handed each of the others a pair of odd-looking goggles, donning a pair himself.

"Clairvoyance goggles," he said.

"Seeing things through ESP?" grunted Barton.

"Right. By clairvoyance many people have seen in their mind's eye startling scenes at a distance through some mysterious psi-channel. Clairvoyance has been called 'mental TV'. What I've done with these goggles is make it a deliberate rather than random event. In short, merely by drawing down psi-power with our tektite helmets, we activate the goggles into clairvoyance to show us everything around us. It requires no light, so we'll be able to see in pitch darkness down at the sea bottom."

Just how far down was it? This they could not know, nor could Brains give any data. Somewhere below lay an ancient land that had once been a thriving society in 35,000 B.C. Even a super-scientific land. That part might be pure legend but not the land itself.

"Ready for astral submersion?"

The other two nodded. The tektite crystal on Hillory's helmet glowed as he suddenly turned wraithlike and dove down into the water. Two more phantom forms followed. They felt no sensation of shock hitting the water nor any sense of chill. There was no choking and gasping from drawing water into their lungs.

In astral form they were divorced from all such physical effects. They glided down swiftly, propelled by their own will power, backed up by psi-energy. When the sunlight faded into a dim greenness and then dark murk, their clairvoyance goggles began working. At first their vision was distorted as they saw surrealistic fish swimming by. But then the scenes clarified into sharper details than any searchlight could supply.

Using psi-intuition—another definite psi-spectrum power latent in every human—Hillory could gauge how far down they were going.

"One mile and still going down," he flashed to his companions via ESP.

"Two miles…nothing in sight"

"Three miles…land ahoy!"

They slowed up as below them spread a vast sunken land of valleys and mountains just as in upper earth. Here and there they discerned temple ruins of stately stone columns and tumbled archways. Huge statuary was also evident. Roadways that were once well-paved and now uptorn still wound beyond the watery horizon.

Hillory even thought he saw the ruins of giant factories and other industrial buildings. A great civilization had once flowered here, all but forgotten, long before the rise of Sumeria and Egypt. Their alien treasure hunt was changing human history or at least shedding light on the darkness of the past.

But they had no time for exploring. Barton and Merry would only be able to hold their astral state for a few hours. They must find the second treasure and be off before then.

"Erosion," gasped Hillory in dismay. "Water erosion for 35,000 years. Even on land most ancient meteorite craters have filled in with loose dirt and crumbling rocks. Down here under water, flows of mud and ooze would long ago have filled the entire pit."

The three halted, confused. "Then we'll never find the spot," said Merry with a disappointed note in her ESP voice.

"Wait," admonished Barton, pointing north. "That wide patch of darkish ooze. It seems to have some sort of high stone wall around it."

As they glided their astral forms overhead, they could distinctly see the lines of the ruins where once immense stone structures had walled off the edge of a pit now filled in.

"We've found it, thanks to the Atlanteans," sang Hillory, cheerfully. "They evidently walled off the pit because it was so hazardous to keep children or grazing animals from falling in. Or maybe it was a famous scenic spot and they ran vehicles along a flat wall to gaze down awed into the gigantic hole. Anyway, there it is. Now we dive down through the mud just as easily as water…

There was just a vague change in temperature and an adjustment required in using the clairvoyant goggles, as they plunged down through the sediment piled up for centuries. No digging machine could ever penetrate to the bottom, but their intangible forms found no barrier to stop them.

"Now to find the treasure container itself," said Hillory. "Just where it will be is hard to say. We don't know the exact bottom of the former pit."

"Then we have to hunt blind," said Barton doubtfully. "It might take hours…days…."

"You should know better than that," returned Hillory easily. "There are psi-tricks for every problem. You've heard of metal detectors up on earth used for finding minerals and ores. I'm going to use a psi-metal detector." Hillory drew down psi-power into his tektite crystal, then mentally fashioned it into electromagnetic radiations that spread in all directions. Quite like a scintillometer, the tektite began to sparkle suddenly as he drifted through the ocean-bottom ooze.

A moment later his clairvoyance goggles spied the huge arm of a buried statue. And in its giant hand was a square metal box exactly like the one they had found on Mount Everest.

Hillory tried to grab the box before he realized his astral hands would only go through it. Then he concentrated on drawing down psi-energy and spraying it over the box until it too turned into a misty astral box.

"The second treasure," exulted Barton as Hillory brought it to them. "Hmm, do you suppose the same thing is inside…."

"Yes," said Hillory who had mentally adjusted his clairvoyance goggles to peer into the metal box. "The same big crystalline globe. The same coiled up strips that look like a tape."

"Ouch," said Barton. "That means like the first one we can't open that crystal globe. It begins to look as if the four spots will give us four strips of tape which are to be spliced together—to do what? Show movies or give us a travelogue of the galaxy?"

"No, I'm sure it's nothing that trivial." Hillory's ESP voice was grave. "I have a hunch—another psi characteristic—that it will be of earth-shaking, or universe-shaking, importance. The deadly eagerness of the mind-alien to get hold of this treasure is another clue to its vast importance." He sighed. "Well, we won't solve that new mystery until we gather all four tapes and get the gem-globes open. Let's go up now, with the box."

Barton glanced upward nervously. "This is about the time for Jorzz to strike. Keep your eyes, or clairvoyant goggles, open."

As they wafted their astral forms up out of the pit and its ooze into the clear ocean water, Merry gave a little ESP screech. "What's coming? That giant wriggling body…it's a sea serpent!"

Undulating its long sinuous body, a fantastic monster was charging them, gaping jaws and sharp teeth open wide.

"Just as he was able to take over the android, Mr. Mind took over the primitive brain of that sea monster," Hillory said rapidly.

"But what are we worried about?" laughed Barton suddenly. "In our astral form, he'll clamp his jaws on nothing—nothing solid. How can he harm us?"

Barton stopped laughing as the sea serpent began to change—into a rippling mistiness.

"Well aware of our astral state," barked Hillory, "Mr. Mind is siccing an astral sea serpent at us. His bite will be just as effective as if we are all in material form. Can you two speed up?"

But Barton and Merry were unable to increase their gliding motion through the water. "We're not experts in using psi-power," gulped Merry. "We're drawing down all we can now. But you can draw more, Thule. You have the treasure box…."

"So get going," yelled Barton.

Hillory's ghost-form did suddenly shoot away. Merry gave a half-sob and Barton stared disbelievingly. I didn't think he'd turn coward...think of his own skin...."

Hillory had dashed upward, pumping psi-power from the tektite. Now he turned and made a feint at the sea serpent's head. Its cruel jaws snapped shut too late. Hillory kept going along the sea serpent's length and then his eyes gleamed. As he suspected, the tail end of the serpent was not wraithlike. Mr. Mind had not taken the trouble to astralize the entire beast when only the head end would be needed to kill.

Glancing about, Hillory saw a hilly slope and rocks at the top. Darting there, he picked a house-sized boulder that was roughly round in shape. Then, sucking in another charge of psi-power, he sent a psi-blast of PK at the rock. Like dice being tumbled about by PK power in ESP experiments at universities, his psi-blow heaved the great stone forward down the slope.

Down it rumbled, though silently to Hillory's psi-ears, and crashed into the tail of the sea serpent, ripping out a huge wound from which blood began to pour. The sea serpent's tail began to lash and writhe in agony, and its head end came swinging around as if to see what had attacked it.

That left Barton and Merry free of menace, and they were already streaking upward. Hillory followed, staring down at the awesome sight of a monster longer than a whale twisting and coiling in its death-throes as its lifeblood poured out, staining the water. The front end of the serpent had now materialized.

"Mr. Mind had to abandon it," said Hillory in satisfaction.

"You won another round in your mental duel with Jorzz," said Barton, admiringly.

But Hillory still had an uneasy feeling, a hunch that their mental enemy had not yet given up. A subtle psi-warning told him that Jorzz was nearby, perhaps working up another menace.

Hillory's psi-voice became urgent. "Hurry," he told the other two. "We still have two miles to go to the ocean surface. Mr. Mind is still around and may pull another trick...."

Then he saw it. A deep-sea fish of fantastic shape, with knobs all over and a row of luminescent spots, came swimming directly toward them. It had two huge eyes that glowed redly in a fixed stare.

And unlike other fish, it did not flee from them but swam boldly in their direction.

"That fish," warned Hillory. "Mr. Mind has taken it over and is projecting a hypnotic stare through those eyes."

Hillory then felt the telepathic command that went with the luminous eyes. "Stop! Go back…back to the deep-sea. Turn back down…down…down…."

With a furious effort of will, Hillory pumped psi-power through his tektite and was able to wrench his eyes away. But to his horror he saw Barton and Merry stop as if in a trance. Their astral forms had turned rigid. And as the hypnotic chant grew stronger, they obediently turned and wafted themselves down—down toward the sea bottom again.

"No, don't do it," came Hillory's ESP yell. "Barton…Merry…listen to me. Don't go down…go up."

For a moment the pair stopped, hesitating. But then the deep-sea fish swam in front of them, fixing them with its large unblinking stare. Within the fish, controlling its movements, the mind-alien sent forth his mesmeric command: "Go down…down…down…."

Hillory groaned as he saw Barton and Merry dive down again. To their doom. Soon now their power to hold onto their astral forms would fade away. They would turn to their normal material forms, three miles deep in the ocean. No human beings could survive there for an instant. They would be immediately crushed by the pressure, even before they had a chance to drown.

Hillory still held the treasure box, which was what Jorzz wanted. Yet even though Hillory had warded off the hypnotic command, he was now forced to turn and also dive down in desperation, hoping to save his companions. Hillory himself was now in danger, having drained so much of his psi-gathering power in the battle against the sea serpent. He too would soon lose his psi-hold on his astral form and turn material.

Then three crushed human bodies would lie on the dark sea bottom, while some squid or other sea creature animated by Jorzz would then snatch away the treasure box.

All this rushed through Hillory's panicky mind as he dove after the wraith forms of Barton and Merry. What could he do against the devilish psi-powers displayed by the mind-alien? How could he break the hypnotic spell?

Inspiration rose out of his whirling thoughts. Setting his astral lips grimly, Hillory increased his speed—not swimming but gliding frictionlessly through the water—and began to overtake the deep-sea fish which was swimming in wide loops in order to periodically turn and face the diving pair, keeping them under hypnotic control.

With a spurt of psi-power, Hillory materialized his two hands and the treasure box, which became heavy metal. Then he swung the non-astral treasure box at the fish, crushing its skull. The fish's two big eyes turned dim and began to glaze. The hypnotic spell broke. Barton and Merry looked around dazedly, as if waking from a deep sleep.

"Go back up," screamed Hillory. "As fast as you can."

Their astral forms flashed upward. Hillory followed a short ways behind, keeping his clairvoyant vision darting in all directions. Frustrated with his hypnotic fish trick, Jorzz might still try to control some shark or other sea creature and attempt another nameless psi-threat.

But all went well as they neared the surface…until Barton began to gasp, "Losing control…can't hold my astral form much longer.…"

CHAPTER 12

Another quandary. Hillory debated a moment, then shot up to the surface and beyond, reaching the hovering psi-bubble where they had "anchored" it in the air. Leaping in and tossing the treasure box aside, Hillory returned to his material form and guided the bubble downward. It went underwater with a splash.

Staring all around swiftly, Hillory saw the struggling form of Barton about fifty feet down, completely materialized and in danger of drowning. Sending the bubble close, Hillory scooped up Barton through the bubble's door, at the same time using PK power to keep the water from rushing in. Moments later the bubble shot clear of the sea, into the air.

"Thought you'd never come up," gasped Merry, flinging herself into the bubble just as her astral form materialized into solidity. Beside her, Barton lay choking and spitting water out of his lungs. He finally sat up, recovered.

"Nearly became a permanent ghost," he bantered. He stared gratefully at Hillory. "Good thing you have a bag of magic psi-tricks."

Hillory could not answer. He sat exhausted, drained of psi-energy and physical energy alike. Using psi-powers was somewhat like running at top speed on foot for miles without letup.

Merry saw the frantic signal in his eyes and took over the task of psi-levitation, barely in time. The bubble had thinned dangerously. Firm again, as Merry drew down psi-energy, the bubble carried them home at a good clip.

Hillory was feeling more himself when they arrived and brought in the treasure box. They had the box cut open as before. Hillory drew out the rainbow-hued crystal globe with the coils of tape inside. "We'll bring this right to Dr. Torreo for safekeeping."

When they strode into Dr. Torreo's lab, Hillory said, "Put this in our fifth dimension cache with the other one."

"But the other one isn't there," returned Torreo.

Hillory jerked. "You mean Jorzz somehow got hold of it there?"

"No, no," said Torreo, breaking into a smile. "Dr. Clyde had me bring it back from the fifth dimension and turn it over to Dr. Cheng, who is trying to open it." Hillory was already on his way. "Any luck, Dr. Cheng?" he asked, coming in the lab door. The dwarfed Oriental had the first treasure globe within a meson-microscope and was peering through an eyepiece. He turned wearily.

"Not so far. I'm examining the interlocked structure of the crystal globe. Even if I can't make indestructible matter, maybe I can take it apart."

"That's a paradox," snorted Barton. "If something is indestructible it can never be taken apart."

Cheng eyed him witheringly. "Indestructible is a relative term. It may be impervious to any known force, yet there may be some energy 'key' that will open it up. I'm looking for that key."

Hillory was worried. "But with the crystal globe here, instead of safe in the fifth dimension, the mind-alien might strike to gain possession."

"Yet you want the globe opened, don't you?" said Cheng testily. "You can't have it both ways."

Hillory smiled weakly. He pondered the dilemma. While he was away finding the other globes, Jorzz might change tactics and seize them at Serendipity Labs. Yet if the treasure globes were kept 'locked up" in the fifth dimension, Dr. Cheng could not search for the "key" to open them. It was not easy to match wits with an invisible mind entity who could strike anywhere as he chose.

Something had to be done about this situation. But what?

Hillory turned to Barton and Merry. "We'll let Brains decipher the third treasure spot tomorrow. Right now, I've got some thinking to do."

Hillory first delivered the second globe to Dr. Torreo and waited until he saw it weirdly vanish, transported to their fifth dimensional "strongbox." Then he went to his lab with the gnawing worry that they were still vulnerable to Jorzz though they had beaten him to two treasure caches so far.

* * * *

Dr. Torreo lay sleeping in his quarters at Serendipity Labs. Each of the scientists had a private bedroom in an adjacent section of the building if their researches kept them tied close to their labs. If not, they had the option of driving to their homes which were scattered in the general vicinity and spend time with their families.

Dr. Torreo was too involved with his dimensional explorations to leave and go home and hence slept in his assigned bedroom. It was late at night and quiet through Serendipity Labs.

No one saw the ectoplasmic form that slowly oozed under the door of Torreo's room and materialized into a manlike shape with two owl eyes. The white form deliberately blew a breath of cold air at the sleeping scientist so that he began to shiver. He woke up to pull the blankets tighter around him.

Then he saw the two glowing eyes in the dark, staring at him intently. Dr. Torreo opened his mouth to yell but no sound came out. Instead, his jaw fell slack and he arose in a trance.

A soft ESP whisper was saying, "Arise, Dr. Torreo…go to your lab…go."

In a somnambulistic state, like a zombie, the scientist went to his lab, followed by a white shadow that kept sibilantly sending telepathic whispers into his mind. Within the lab, the ESP voice gave instructions: "Retrieve the treasure globe from the fifth dimension." Obediently, Dr. Torreo began powering up his dimension probe. But as magnetic forces began to build up, they affected Torreo's nervous system, interfering with his catatonic state. His eyes unglazed. His brain resisted the hypnotic command.

He whirled, seeing the ectoplasmic form with its staring eyes. "The mind-alien," he cried. "Trying to get hold of the treasure globe, through me. But I'm prepared…."

Torreo snatched up a pistol that lay hidden on a workbench. He fired pointblank at the white figure. Nothing happened. Torreo emptied the gun in growing alarm.

"Fool," Jorzz hissed sibilantly into his mind from the unmoving white form. "Bullets and all other such weapons cannot harm a psi-creature."

"No, but this can." The lights snapped on and Hillory stood by the switch, aiming a tubular device with a tektite crystal mounted on its barrel. With a whooshing sound, a faint pink ray streaked out and struck the ectoplasmic form. With a soundless puff, it vanished.

"I was waiting for you, Jorzz," said Hillory. "I figured you would try the hypno-trick on Dr. Torreo, to make him withdraw the treasure globes—Dr. Cheng returns his each night too—from the fifth dimension. My psi-weapon can't harm you, but it can disrupt your control over anything you animate. Clear?"

Something very much like a bitter curse floated back as the mind-alien left, its ESP aura fading away.

Dr. Torreo was white and shaken. Hillory gave him a glass of water, then explained. "In my lab before, I devised this psi-pistol. I've given it a psi-charge of power that will last for many shots of PK 'dynamite.' You'll keep this gun on hand all the time, Dr. Torreo. If Jorzz attempts any more tricks on you, fire away."

The color returned to Torreo's face, and he managed a weak smile. "Thanks. I'll feel much safer with this, Hillory."

Hillory paused at the door. "Tomorrow morning I'm giving Dr. Cheng a psi-pistol too. Furthermore, I'll have the machine shop turn out more and arm every man in the place, including the janitor, night-watchman, and service people."

Hillory went to bed, feeling better. The psi-pistols would make Serendipity Labs mind-proof from Jorzz's machinations. The treasure hunt trips might be a different story, but here at the labs the mind-alien would not be able to use his animating schemes to harass them.

Bit by bit, Hillory reflected in satisfaction; he was weaving a net of defense against the fantastic alien mind from outer space. Somehow, he had to win out in this unprecedented battle of mentalities using almost magical psi phenomena and paranormal powers.

But so many nagging questions remained. Why was Jorzz after the treasure from space? Would they be able to find the other treasure tapes, hidden an age ago? What would the strange tapes reveal? Most crucial of all—would they ever get the adamant globe containers open to retrieve the tapes?

And a final chilling thought stole into Hillory's mind. Would the mental mastermind from space find some other weird way to gain his goal?

REJECTED flashed the light of the computer for the 8th time.

Barton's mustache twitched. "Brains doesn't like any of the maps of ancient earth we've showed so far. The one for Mount Everest worked only because that part of the world was correctly cartographed. And the map showing Atlantis allowed him to pinpoint spot No. 2. But some other map is needed to reveal spot No. 3."

"We're going to run out of maps," muttered Hillory, handing over another one. "Merry's only holding two more."

But this time the lighted screen read: ACCEPTABLE. Then, for solving time at Barton's request: 14 MINUTES, 2 SECONDS.

"At last the right map," sighed Hillory.

"Wait," said Barton surprised. "Here's the map you just handed me. By mistake, I put in one of the maps we previously tried." Barton frowned. "I don't get it. Why would Brains first reject that map, then accept it?"

Hillory shrugged. "Maybe Brains didn't scan it right the first time."

Barton glowered. "Computers don't pull dumb boners like that."

"Figure it out later. Right now, let's see if Brains will give us spot No. 3."

When the time was up, Barton pressed the voice button. His eyebrows shot up as a confused babble came from the computer, a gibberish of incomprehensible syllables.

"Brains sounds incoherent," said Barton, astonished. "This never happened before…."

Then, with a faint click, the computer delivered normal words. "Sorry. A brief circuit mix-up. Reporting on the ancient map of earth, in comparison to the alien map, spot No. 3 is revealed. It is in the Amazon Jungle."

"But that's an enormous area," remonstrated Barton.

"Just where in the jungle? Have you determined the latitude and longitude?"

"That was not possible due to discrepancies between the metal map and the comparison map. However, an analog interpretation gives the spot as being 933 miles due west of the mouth of the Amazon River."

"That's still too generalized," muttered Barton. "The mouth of the Amazon is wide, and the spot might be miles north or south of the point 933 miles to the west. Any further refinement of the data?"

This last was addressed to the computer, but it signaled a negative.

"Guess that's the best Brains can do in this case," Hillory said to the others. "It'll be something of a blind search with no markers or landmarks to go by, just featureless jungle land."

"Still, the alien pirates who buried the treasure tape there wouldn't just stick it in the middle of plain jungles," observed Merry. "Maybe we'll hit on some outstanding rock or peculiar cliff or something."

"Something's funny about this," said Barton broodingly, his thoughts on something else. Suddenly he snapped on the voice circuit again. "Brains, why did you first reject this map, then accept it?"

There was a moment of silence from the computer, as if it were collecting its thoughts. Then: "There was a crease in the earth map the first time, distorting the configuration of the land masses involved. The crease was absent the second time, and the map became useful."

Barton grinned with a red face. "I can almost hear Brains say under his breath—*watch it next time, fumble-fingers.*"

"The Amazon it is," said Hillory briskly. "We'll wear appropriate clothing. And we'd better take along weapons, rifles as well as the laser-gun. And this time we may need food and water for a week."

CHAPTER 13

The next day their psi-bubble flyer hissed through the air and sped southward. They passed the Panama Canal and soon the upper edges of the wild Amazon jungle hove into view below.

"Brazil has done a good job of clearing some of the jungle land and converting it into cattle ranges," commented Hillory. "But much of it is un-reclaimed. "It's still the wildest patch of tropical jungle on earth."

Under Hillory's guidance, the psi-bubble swung to the eastern edge of South America until they hung over the wide mouth of the Amazon. Barton then used the Pathfinder to take a due west course for 933 miles. Finally the bubble lowered and began making a slow spiral that kept broadening out.

"Keep your eyes open for any oddity down there," said Hillory. "Anything unusual that the aliens may have considered a marker of some kind."

Some minutes later, Merry pointed down. "There. A distinct patch of red rock. It stands out like a sore thumb from the uniform greenery of the surrounding jungle."

"Might be," agreed Barton. "Lower and let's look around."

The bubble descended to the ground in the middle of the red rock clearing. It was not entirely barren. Where the rock had crumbled, a few trees had taken root. One old gnarled oak towered some two hundred feet high.

"Could that tree be the marker for the exact spot?" wondered Barton.

"A tree 35,000 years old?" scoffed Merry.

"I'm brilliant today," grunted Barton. He tipped his sun helmet to wipe his brow. "Whew. Plenty hot and humid here."

"This shade looks good," said Merry, looking wilted as she stepped under the giant oak. She looked up and froze. Sitting on a branch and about to spring was a jaguar, its ferocious eyes fastened on its intended victim. Fear paralyzed her throat. The great cat leaped.

But it was met in mid-leap by a sharp hiss. A ruby red ray stabbed through its heart. To the side stood Barton, holding his laser-gun. Merry was unable to scramble aside and the dead beast's body fell on her, pinning her down. Hillory ran to her aid and dragged the corpse off her.

She got to her feet shakily, otherwise unhurt. Barton holstered his gun but yanked it out again as the sinuous coils of a huge python swung down from the branches toward Hillory and the girl. A coil wrapped around them before Barton could take careful aim and drill a hole through its head. The serpentine length of the snake then dangled down limply with its tail still twined in the branches.

Hillory peered carefully into the branches. "Seems there are no more killer beasts up there."

"Two is enough," said Merry, shuddering. She sat down weakly trembling. Hillory turned at an odd sound, like thudding hooves. He gave an amazed grunt to see a huge armadillo charging out of the jungle. Barton had his back turned, and this time it was Hillory who snapped up his rifle and fired. The armadillo thundered closer, then stopped dead in its tracks and toppled over.

Barton stared at the big carcass. "Must be a water hole nearby where those critters live. But why would he deliberately charge us when we didn't disturb him?"

Hillory had a baffled look in his eye. "And the jaguar and python. They seldom attack humans unless they are cornered or extremely starved."

His lips tightened. "Three killer beasts attacking us the moment we arrive. It all seems unreal, unnatural. It smacks of being staged… by *Jorzz*."

"Just what I was thinking," nodded Barton, plucking at his mustache. "Well, he's probably run out of killer beasts near enough to menace us."

They were all sitting under the oak in its shade now, recovering from the rapid-fire series of animal attacks. Hillory felt uneasy somehow. Would more danger show up, engineered by the cunning mind-alien? In what form?

Merry clutched his arm. "That shadow...of a tree branch...it's *moving*!"

Too late they glanced up. Tree branches began to whip downward toward them, though there was no wind.

"Jorzz animated this tree now," gasped Hillory. "Run for it."

But as they tried to stumble away, they were still under the widespread lower branches of the tree, which bent downward and formed a barrier. Wherever they turned, more branches swung down to hem them in. Then one branch with many stems whipped down and "seized" them.

It was the only word. The branch acted like a huge leafy hand, its stems curling around them. They were lifted off their feet. Then, as the branch whipped back upward, they were tossed higher and higher in the tree.

Like well-trained appendages, the broad branches kept flinging the three helpless people higher and higher.

Barton managed to get his laser-gun in hand and shot wildly. "No use," he yelled. "How can you kill a tree?"

"We're being tossed to the top of the tree," said Hillory, getting the words out jerkily during their violent motion upward.

"And at the top?" said Merry, horrified.

"We'll be flung down all the way to the ground...onto hard red rock," answered Barton, starkly.

Hillory had pulled a psi-tektite from his pocket. Even in his wild gyrations among the tossing branches, he forced it in front of his eyes and strained to draw psi-energy from it. There wasn't much time now. Their three forms were twisting through the air and drawing close to the tree's tip.

Suddenly, a blinding flash materialized out of nowhere. It struck the base of the tree and split it open with a thunderous report.

Immediately, the tree's branch movements became a wild, uncoordinated thrashing, like a dying man with twisting limbs. Branches no longer flipped them upward but let them drop.

"Grab that thick branch directly below us, and crawl toward the trunk of the tree," yelled Hillory. It was a mad scramble, but they made it. Then they clung to the sturdy trunk and watched the thrashing tree branches subside into limpness.

"That's how to kill a tree," said Barton during the climb down. "With lightning."

"Psi-lightning," amended Hillory. "It wasn't cloud-made but came directly out of thin air from a clot of psi-power I formed. But Jorzz very nearly had us there."

On the ground, they saw that the tree was truly dead with its roots blackened where they had tom spasmodically out of the soil. "But why couldn't the mind-alien still animate the tree, even when dead, like he did with the yeti?"

"Too much psi-energy required," answered Hillory. "Jorzz is limited in how much psi-power he can draw down and utilize. He's only able to cause short bursts of activity in the things he animates."

"Luckily for us," breathed Merry. She brightened. "Well, after that rude interruption, let's find the treasure cache here."

"There is none," said Barton gloomily.

They stared at him.

"This was a wild goose chase," continued Barton. He kicked away a stone in disgust. "We got our instructions from Jorzz, not my computer."

"Huh?" said Merry.

Barton faced them, blazing anger in his eyes. "I mean that Jorzz slipped his free-mind into my computer circuits and cooked up a false treasure spot to waste our time—or lead us into a death trap. Jorzz guessed that a jungle would offer him plenty of killers to animate against us."

"But how do you know Jorzz 'animated' the computer?" Hillory wanted to know, stunned.

"I should have suspected it from the start," growled Barton, giving his mustache a sharp tweak. "The way Brains first sounded incoherent, probably because Jorzz was having trouble manipulating the voice circuits. Then the vague location without geographical coordinates. Brains would never be that sloppy about it. And finally, Brains first rejecting and then accepting the same map."

"But he explained about the crease...."

"Crease, my foot. Brains has an automatic crease smoother for any paper he is to scan. It slipped my dumb mind until now."

Hillory sagged. "Taken in like fools. Jorzz almost did lure us to our death. Even so, he wasted our time at a false spot No. 3. Well, back we go in the psi-bubble."

"With our tails between our legs," said Barton wryly.

Anger flashed from Merry's brown eyes. "When I think of all the sun tan lotion and bug-bite spray I carefully packed up...." A stream of phrases came spitting from her lips.

"Come again?" said Barton. "Those sound like cuss-words."

"Yes, but in foreign languages. That way people still think I'm too much of a lady to swear."

* * * *

Hillory reported in to Dr. Clyde about their abortive mission to the Amazon. The director scowled. "A devilish trick on the part of Jorzz. It delays our final solution of the great mystery. And it's keeping you from resuming your psi researches."

"Not really," mused Hillory. "I've learned more about using psi-powers than ever before, through battling the mind-alien."

Hillory left and dropped in at Dr. Cheng's lab. "Any luck in breaking open the treasure globes?"

"Not yet," conceded the oriental dwarf. "Every avenue of approach I've used ends up nowhere. Even a bombardment of high-speed protons that would disrupt steel armor has no effect on the rainbow crystal."

Hillory felt perturbed as he left. If they never succeeded in opening the strange containers, they would never know the secret of the treasure tapes. That would be a bitter ending for their hazardous treasure hunt all over earth, courting danger at every step.

At Dr. Torreo's lab, Hillory asked for the metal map back. It had been stored, during his absence, in the fifth dimension, along with one of the two treasure globes. The metal scroll materialized in Torreo's device.

When Hillory entered the computer lab, Barton was busy hooking up wires to one console. "That fixes that. Jorzz won't be able to sneak into Brains and tamper with his circuits. Here, let's test it. Hillory, you stand near the console and send a telepathic message to Brains. Say anything like...oh, copper is colored purple."

Hillory took out his psi-tektite and concentrated on the mental message. Instantly, a bright red bulb near Barton lit up and a bell clanged. Also the computers lighted screen flashed the word *interference*.

"Fine," said Hillory, handing over the metal scroll. "Now to solve for spot No. 3 again." He frowned. "The trouble is, we have only two ancient maps of earth left. Brains rejected the other eight…."

"No, he didn't." Merry came in, her arms loaded with maps. "It was Jorzz who falsely rejected them in order to pull his stunt."

"That's right," said Hillory, brightening. "We can run through them again with a good chance of hitting the right one."

It was only the third map that Barton fed into the computer which brought acceptance, and the answer was delivered in nine minutes.

"Comparison of the ancient earth map and the alien map indicates that spot No. 3 is a deep cave in Africa." Brains gave the exact latitude and longitude. Then he concluded: "I vaguely detect from the text that markings in that labyrinth of caves will lead to the treasure itself." Hillory sent Merry running to the library for a modern map of Africa in detail. When she returned, he pinpointed the spot according to the computer's data.

"There it is. It's called the Cave of Idols today, in Ghana. We can set out today in the psi-bubble. We'll take along good electric lamps as the cave will be dark."

"We may need passports too," pointed out Merry. "That cave is a showplace for tourists. The local officials and guards won't like us simply dropping down from the sky without sanction, violating their air space and illegally entering their country."

Barton made a sour face. "Getting passports and visas and all that claptrap—ugh. It would be a big delay, and we might never get permission."

CHAPTER 14

Hillory fretted at this new problem. Before, in going to Mount Everest and the Amazon, he had fleetingly thought of following protocol, then dismissed it as unimportant since they would be far from any centers of civilization. And the descent to Atlantis had required no legal papers in the free ocean.

But now, landing in a populous country at one of their scenic wonders and blithely walking in to explore for a "treasure" would only land them in trouble neck deep. The only way to get permission would be for Dr. Clyde to put pressure on Washington. But the only way to do that would be to reveal their whole secret project to the government.

It would be like stirring a hornet's nest. The repercussions might well rob them of the rewards and take the treasure hunt out of their hands. Hillory faced the other two, knowing they were thinking the same.

"Why stick our necks out? All large natural caverns, they say, have more than one entrance or exit. So we'll simply avoid the main entrance where the guide tours are conducted and find some obscure entrance. Most big caves have many branches and miles of passageways. The place where the idols of some past civilization are on display would occupy only a small portion of the caverns."

"So we sneak in like smugglers," grinned Barton.

"Illegal entry and all that," chirped Merry.

They smiled at one another like conspirators. It seemed so trivial in the face of the tantalizing riddle of outer space they were struggling to solve. What did a few fussy earth laws and routine conventions mean in comparison to a treasure buried 35,000 years ago, long before the idols had ever been installed in the cave or the country taken over by people?

Without a trace of a guilty conscience, they embarked. Within an hour the psi-bubble was descending over Ghana, to a wasteland section where the Cave of Idols existed. They had deliberately chosen the nighttime.

"There won't be any guided tours going on," said Hillory. "Only a guard or two at the main entrance. And darkness won't inhibit our search for another entrance—not with the clairvoyance goggles."

Again they wore the goggles that by some queer paranormal process could peer anywhere and reveal details in sharp clarity. They could extend the range simply by willing their "mental TV" to pick up more distant scenes. They scanned the terrain below as the psi-bubble slowly drifted past the archway of the main entrance.

"Wait," said Hillory. "Set your range within the main cave. The goggles can see through rock, you know. Take a look at what the tourists see."

"And without paying the admission fee," chuckled Barton like a gleeful child sneaking into an exhibit.

They sobered and stared in awe at what their clairvoyant pickup revealed. Within a giant cavern with a lofty ceiling studded with stalactites stood a row of huge stone idols, each twenty feet tall. Some lost civilization had painstakingly chiseled out these idols in grotesque forms that were half-man and half-beast. Each idol's eyes were enormous sparkling gems of fabulous worth. It was no wonder that it was a strong tourist attraction.

"Time to get down to business," said Hillory. "I'll guide the bubble over what would be the back of the cave from which tunnels would branch. Somewhere there should be a side entrance, even if it's just a small hole."

Below lay typical "badlands" that were often associated with caves. Distorted rock formations lay twisted all over with a few straggling trees and bushes rooted here and there. A bleak stone wilderness carved by nature's tools through the ages.

Merry clutched Hillory's arm. "Down there. A black hole. It goes down through the rock."

"One of the cave's vent-holes," said Hillory. "We're in luck."

The bubble landed and they stepped out near the hole, snapping on their flash-lamps. "Raise your clairvoyance goggles," said Hillory. "Direct vision is better when the footing is uncertain."

Hillory went down first, finding footholds in the rocky hole which did not drop straight down but slanted. Thirty feet down he stood in a large passageway and waited till the other two had joined him. Further on, their lamps revealed several branch tunnels.

"People spend days and weeks exploring caves," said Merry, dismayed. "How do we know just where the aliens hid the treasure? We might blunder around and get nowhere."

"You forget," put in Barton, "that Brains said the aliens left guide markings in the cave."

"What kind?"

"Who knows?" answered Hillory for Barton. "Just keep your eyes open for any unusual marking on the stone walls."

But before they went on, he tied one end of a string around a small stalagmite and let it unwind from a reel strapped to his belt. "A trick borrowed from the Minotaur legend. We want to be sure to find our way back through these confusing labyrinths."

Eerie silence surrounded them except for their footfalls as they trudged along the dusty passageways. They wound erratically in all directions, sometimes going up and down. At branch corridors, Hillory pretended to flip a coin and chose one at random.

Merry gave a little scream as a small dark shape flitted past. "Bats! But then, what can you expect in caves?"

Further along a passageway opened out into a large cavern with uprearing stalagmites. Glinting stalactites hung precariously from the roof, poised as if to drop like spears and impale those beneath.

"Don't worry," soothed Barton at the girl's fearful stare. "They're formed by limestone drippings and are solidly affixed to the stone ceiling…."

At that moment a loud crack reverberated through the hollow cavern. Hillory's flashlight caught the moving glint above.

"A stalactite broke loose," he yelled, jerking Merry back. The massive stone spear with a sharp point struck barely a yard away, splintering and sending flying rubble at them as they shielded their faces.

"Our little playmate—Jorzz," growled Barton. "Up to his mischievous mayhem again."

"I'm afraid so," hissed Hillory. "He used PK power to break off that stalactite. Don't walk directly under them anymore."

All of them glanced around in dread wondering what threat would be hurled at them next by the murderous mind from outer space. A dark cave deep within the bowels of earth was the ideal place for uncanny psi-ambushes.

But their worry was replaced by excitement as Merry's flash limelighted a peculiar marking on the stone wall—three bones in a crossed pattern.

"The same marking as on that flying saucer we found."

"I should have known," said Hillory. "It's a sort of skull-and-crossbones emblem used by the pirates who buried the split-up treasure tapes."

"We hit it at a cross corridor," pointed out Barton. "They came from another passageway than we did. But now we can just follow their markings to the treasure spot."

"But which way?" asked Merry and Barton looked both ways, uncertainly. "We don't know which way the pirates came," she continued. "One way will simply backtrack them and lead out of the caves."

Hillory stared closely at the marking. "Hmm. The three crossbones are tilted as if to point the way to where they hid the treasure. We'll follow them that way. If I'm wrong, it only means we have to retrace our steps back to here and go the other way."

They followed the emblems tilted forward, which were marked wherever passageways crossed or the way was uncertain. Suddenly, Hillory halted at a pile of stone that filled the next corridor.

"A cave-in," groaned Barton. "It happened in the 35,000 years since the pirates came here."

They stared in dismay at the heap of broken stone that blocked their way. "Not even a chink for an ant to crawl through," said Merry, frustratedly.

"This calls for some psi-blasting," sighed Hillory, remembering how it had drained him of psi-energy when destroying the yeti on Mount Everest. But there was no help for it. Using his psi-tektite, he again frowned in deep concentration, routing psi-power from the all-pervasive psi-pool of the universe through the crystal.

There was a sizzling sound in the air, and Hillory motioned the others to stand back and huddle down. Then came an explosive sound as some awesome para-force drilled through the rock pile with irresistible power.

"Neat job," crowed Barton, running forward. He had to stoop to get through the hole formed, but he beckoned the others. Hillory came last, his feet dragging, feeling as if he had climbed a mountain. His psi-reservoir was nearly drained, leaving a physical tiredness in every part of his body. Such were the penalties of handling gross amounts of psi-power.

Merry paused to take his arm and help him along while Barton eagerly ran ahead. His yelp came back to them. "Here's the treasure!"

Rounding a bend in the passageway, Hillory and the girl saw Barton near a niche in the wall, marked with a huge crossbones emblem. He reached in and withdrew what lay within the niche.

"The same many-colored crystal globe with coiled tape inside, naturally. Only one more tape to go and we have all four. Then, *if* we get the globes open and *if* we find out how to 'play' the tapes, we'll know what the 'treasure' is—if any."

"A lot of 'ifs' to this," nodded Merry. "Just what could tapes that space pirates buried so elaborately lead to? What sort of 'treasure' could it be?"

"That's an odd thought," pondered Hillory. "Apparently the tapes themselves are not the 'treasure'—or are they? It seems rather silly for pirates to bury tapes that would only lead to the real treasure somewhere, else. Maybe the tapes are really it, in some unfathomable way."

"Let's stop gabbing and get out of here," put in Barton nervously. "If Jorzz is invisibly following us and saw us find the treasure tape, he'll strike again. Let's not give him too much time."

Barton picked up the string that Hillory had unwound and began following it by hand, without reeling it in. As they went along in the cathedral silence, Hillory's sixth sense warned him that the mind-alien was near. His pulse increasing, he peered warily ahead, hoping to anticipate whatever deadly surprise lay ahead. It was almost certain that Jorzz would strike at them now....

Faintly, they heard a thumping sound, vaguely resembling ponderous footsteps. Looking blankly at one another they went on, reaching the huge rock chamber they had traversed before. Halfway across, they stood rooted in dread as the heavy footsteps became loud. Then they saw it—a towering stone figure.

"Jorzz animated one of the stone idols," gasped Hillory, almost in disbelief. "Tons and tons of rock. By some weird psi-manipulation of matter, he made the stone legs become temporarily flexible so that it could walk on them without breaking apart."

Their way was blocked and they darted toward the other side of the giant cavern, only to stop in horror. Before them lay a wide gorge in the cave floor, whose shadowy depths seemed to have no bottom.

"We can't jump it," panted Barton, panic in his voice. "Trapped… trapped between the stone idol and a deep pit."

They huddled at the edge of the crevasse, staring in terror at the great stone idol as it stumped forward like a juggernaut. Hillory held his tektite and tried desperately to summon up a psi-blast.

"Can't make it," he muttered. "Too drained…"

"Your laser-gun, Jim," screeched Merry. "Use it."

Barton pulled it out, wondering why he had not thought of it immediately. He fired, blasting a neat hole in the stone idol's middle… but it kept coming.

"Naturally it can't 'die' or be wounded," gulped Barton. "I'll concentrate on one leg and try to cut it off."

He fired again and again, the ruby-red beam hissing like an angry snake. A series of holes appeared, running across the idol's leg but not enough to sever it. It kept stomping toward them like a behemoth.

CHAPTER 15

But meanwhile, Hillory had noticed a huge stalactite near them, whose base was worn thin. Holding his tektite, he strained to produce one more psi-blast. It was a weak one but it cracked the base and the stalactite fell with a crash—directly in front of the idol's lumbering feet.

As the three tiny humans huddled to the side, they saw the giant stone figure stumble and fall, pitching headlong into the huge crevasse. The falling idol vanished, and seconds later they heard a deafening rumble from far below where it landed, broken to bits.

"That was a narrow squeak," shuddered Barton. "Jorzz meant to have the idol stamp us flat under his stone feet."

"He failed to get this," said Hillory exultantly, holding up the treasure globe.

"But let's hurry out of this horrid place," said Merry in a trembling voice. She caught up the guiding string and followed it hand over hand as the other two followed, lighting the way with their flash-lamps. The rest of the trip seemed routine.

But when they came to the high-domed cavern hung with sharp stalactites, one of them broke off and hurled down at them, as a sort of farewell shot from Jorzz it seemed. Merry's scream warned them in time to dodge. But as the stalactite shattered, one long sliver lanced through the air and struck Barton, piercing his chest. He fell, groaning. Merry knelt at his side then, looked up at Hillory in horror. It was a fatal wound.

Hillory's insides twisted into a knot. He felt responsible for Barton's coming death. If he had not insisted on carrying through this mad game of alien treasure-hunting, it would not have happened. Now a life would be taken, the life of young brilliant Jim Barton.

Hillory cringed as he seemed to hear silent laughter in the air, the psychic mockery of their enemy, Jorzz. How had he hoped to beat the mind-alien, who could strike invisibly with his fantastic psi-tricks?

"I—I'm done for," gasped Barton, blood trickling out of the corner of his mouth. "Don't waste time. Go…let me die here…."

"You won't die," said Hillory, in sudden firmness, a strange gleam in his eye. "I'll beat Jorzz at this game too."

Merry stared at him, wondering if his mind were slipping. "We can't get him to a hospital in less than an hour!" she whispered. "He won't last that long."

"Just get him to the psi-bubble outside," ordered Hillory. "You lead the way, following the string. I'll carry him."

Hoisting Barton carefully over his shoulder, Hillory stumbled along in the uneven footing of the caves. Barton moaned with pain at the jogging and then passed out, to Hillory's relief. After what seemed an eternity, they climbed up out of the slanting hole by which they had entered. It was still night.

As soon as they were safely in the rising psi-bubble, Hillory rapidly ripped Barton's jacket and shirt off, exposing the wound with the end of the stone sliver still sticking up. Gripping the tip, he slowly withdrew it.

"But that will only make him bleed freely," said Merry, aghast. "Thule, have you lost your reason? Barton might have had a chance if we had rushed him to the nearest hospital here in Africa—"

She broke off and turned her horrified eyes away as blood came spouting out of the raw wound after the splinter was drawn out. Hillory now took out his tektite crystal and began concentrating.

Merry stared, half in pity. "What good will that do you? Psi-tricks can't help a dying man."

Hillory said nothing. He had recovered somewhat from his previous draining of psi-energy. Still, sweat beaded his brow as he forced himself to gather more psi-energy. But now he was going to do something different with it, something much greater than before. Something nearly magical….

Merry heard a grunt from Hillory, and then she stared in utter disbelief. The bleeding from Barton's wound had abruptly stopped. Still more astoundingly, the edges of the wound began to constrict as if they were rapidly *healing*.

Hillory suddenly collapsed and fell back with a low moan. "Can't carry it any further…played out…but I think Barton will live."

"Psychogenesis!" said Merry suddenly. "One of the psi-phenomena marked on your chart. You used psi-healing, in other words."

Hillory nodded weakly. "Never tried it before. Based on those cases of people with terminal cancer who suddenly get well or on men badly wounded in war who miraculously healed up. Somehow, they had tapped the great psi-pool and subconsciously converted the psi-energy into killing off cancer cells or in creating and building up new body cells inside a wound. The evidence was there."

He glanced at Barton, who was breathing more easily now in his unconscious state. "In the case of Barton, I commanded his veins and arteries to close off, first. Then the body's healing mechanism was told to accelerate. Psi-energy made it happen, at least partially."

"Think what this can mean to doctors," breathed Merry, eyes shining. "Lives saved by psychogenesis. Maybe amputated arms and legs re-grown even. People cured of fatal ailments…."

"Let's not dream too far," admonished Hillory; "It will take a long time to convince the establishment that it isn't fakery. Look how they've rejected all faith healings, which are really inadvertent applications of psi-genesis. Then it will take a longer time for doctors to develop psi-skills for healing. Remember it's taken me ten years to even begin using psi-powers."

Barton's eyes opened suddenly. He sat up, with infinite bewilderment stamped on his face. "I don't feel like I'm dying now. Why do I feel so good? Why do I feel as if my wound is healing?"

"Because it is," laughed Merry, briefly telling him of Hillory's remarkable feat.

Surprise spread over Barton's face as if it would stay there forever. "You pulled me back from the dead. Saved my life."

"Take it easy," said Hillory, flushing at the awed gratitude in Barton's eyes. "Your wound hasn't fully healed yet. And by the way, I feel like a surgeon who forgot to suture the patient's wound. I'll finish the job back at Serendipity Labs after I've recharged my psi-batteries, so to speak."

* * * *

Dr. Clyde ran his finger over the smooth skin on Barton's chest "Completely healed," he marveled. "All in one hour."

Hillory put aside his tektite crystal. "Now don't go yelling this from the rooftops, or Serendipity Labs will be mobbed as the faith-healing center of the world. Like all other scientific discoveries and processes, this must be thoroughly investigated for years before the technique can be given to medical science."

Clyde nodded soberly. "We can't go off half psi-cocked."

"Besides," piped up Barton, "we still have to finish our alien treasure-hunt. I'm perfectly well and able to go for No. 4. I feel fine." He danced a little jig, then took Hillory's hand. "I'm a dead man come alive, living on borrowed time—thanks to you."

"Spend some of your borrowed time with Brains now," said Hillory, to hide his embarrassment, "to locate the fourth and final spot. Then we'll have the complete four-part alien treasure tape."

"That is," came the voice of Dr. Cheng who had just come in, "if we ever succeed in opening these globe-crystals." He held up one, and his oriental face looked sad.

"Did you try smashing two of them together?" asked Merry. "Maybe the only thing that will crack open that super-hard object is another super-hard object."

The little scientist stared at her as if stunned. Then he galloped out as if driven by devils.

"You may have given him the big breakthrough he needed," Hillory said to Merry. "But let's get on with our job. Merry, have Dr. Torreo bring back the metal map from the fifth dimension. Then bring our remaining ancient earth maps to Barton's lab."

The computer stubbornly refused map after map until Merry handed the last one to Barton. "If that doesn't work, we're sunk. Nobody else in the world has devised any other map for earth of 35,000 B.C."

They waited anxiously for Brains to give his decision. The lights flashed—REJECTED. They all groaned. But then the computer placed another message on the screen—PICTURE OF EARTH IS INCOMPLETE.

"Incomplete?" echoed Barton. "What does that mean? If you have all the ancient oceans and land masses in place, plus the presumed icecaps, what else is needed for a global map of earth?"

"Hmm, I wonder," mused Hillory, a thought stealing into his mind. "Earth is composed of the mesosphere down inside, and the lithosphere at its surface. But a true picture should include the *atmo-sphere* around it."

Hillory sent Merry to the drafting room where drawings were made on order for scientific projects. She returned with a new kind of earth map, one that showed earth as a globe in space, with most of the land masses and seas below hidden by clouds. But the atmosphere was marked in, broken down into its prime layers—troposphere, stratosphere, ionosphere, and the final magnetosphere that stretched out for thousands of miles into empty space. The Van Allen doughnut belts were also marked in around the equator.

"But what is going to come out of that?" queried Barton, puzzled. "How can this pinpoint another spot on earth? Well, here goes."

He fed the new "map" to Brains, along with the alien map. Instantly the lighted sign showed acceptance and gave an eight-minute solving time.

Hardly a word was spoken among the tense people waiting. As before, others had stolen in caught by this breathless saga of space—Clyde, Argyle, Torreo, Cheng, and Yonah. They were almost as much involved as the trio of adventurers who had brought back three of the treasure globes.

At last Brains boomed forth his answer: "The fourth treasure spot is above earth, in an artificial satellite."

"Wow, what a surprise," murmured Barton, pressing the hold-button for a moment. But he saw by Hillory's face that he had expected it.

Barton let Brains go on. "The satellite is tiny. In fact, it is a crystal globe like the others, orbiting by itself. Questions?"

"What kind of orbit?" demanded Barton.

"Equatorial. Exactly."

"Altitude of orbit?"

"Twenty-three thousand five hundred statute miles."

"The well-known stationary orbit," said Hillory. "Like those of the telcom satellites used for worldwide relay of TV and radio signals. They're called 24-hour orbits, matching earth's rotation. Once placed in the precise position over the equator, the satellite stays fixed at one spot above earth. Naturally, the alien pirates would choose that sort of stable position so they could easily find the satellite when they returned."

"But they never did," added Merry. "Which leaves it up to us to retrieve this satellite treasure No. 4."

"But why," spoke up Clyde, "was this satellite never discovered if it was orbiting earth for 35,000 years, long before America or Russia sent up space vehicles?"

"Too high up and too small," returned Hillory. "It's difficult for even radar to spot a comsat at that height unless its position is known. The position is pinpointed actually by the radio signals that the comsat is constantly picking up and relaying. So a tiny object the size of a grapefruit—shades of Khrushchev!—that sends down no tracking signals could easily escape detection by all our tracking networks. Anyway, it's there, unknown to the world at large."

Barton turned Brains back on. "One more question. What spot over earth was the treasure satellite placed?"

"Over the tallest peak in the largest land mass that lies across the equator."

"The largest land mass across the equator," said Merry promptly, "is Africa. And the tallest peak there is Mount Kilimanjaro in Tanzania, almost 20,000 feet high."

"That gives us an easy landmark to find," said Hillory. "We have enough information now to pick up No. 4."

"But can your psi-bubble take you into space itself?" Clyde looked dubious.

"No problem there," said Hillory easily. "We can beef up the psi-bubble to hold air as tightly as an astronaut's craft. Of course we'll take along plenty of bottled oxygen as reserves. If you supply those by tomorrow morning, Dr. Clyde, we'll start then."

"The last leg," breathed Barton, eyes afire. "The home stretch. Then we'll have all four parts of the treasure tape."

"And maybe this time," said Merry gaily, "we'll have a quiet trip. What can Jorzz animate in *empty space*?"

They all grinned—too soon.

CHAPTER 16

"That meteor!" screamed Merry, pointing out of the bubble-wall. "Coming straight at us."

"Big as a washtub," choked Barton. "Can it crush the psi-bubble?"

"I'd hate to test that out," admitted Hillory. "At meteoric speed of some 60,000 miles a second, it would probably smash through our bubble just as through a spacecraft's hard metal walls. It's Jorzz's handiwork again. He somehow deflected the high-speed meteoroid and aimed it straight for us."

Merry had detected the meteoroid with her clairvoyant goggles from a considerable distance. This gave them time to see it coming, rapidly enlarging, a big jagged stone slowly tumbling as it rushed through space.

Hillory was already using his tektite to concentrate and shove the psi-bubble aside. But to his alarm, the meteoroid also turned slightly, again on a collision course with them.

"Jorzz is guiding it like a missile," yelled Barton hoarsely, watching in his clairvoyant goggles. "Thule, can you avoid it?"

Hillory used psi-power to fling the bubble in different directions but the oncoming meteoroid matched every maneuver with deadly precision.

Only split seconds were left now before impact. But Hillory had shot a telepathic command to his two companions. The space cannonball struck the psi-bubble with its three passengers…but only passed through three wraithlike figures sitting in a misty ball.

Merry looked at Hillory as they began to materialize again. "Thank heaven you gave us that telepathic tip-off to turn into our astral forms. The meteoroid went through nothing that was tangible in the normal universe."

"And though our psi-bubble collapsed, I simply created a new one around us," said Hillory.

Barton still looked shaken up. "If Jorzz throws more meteoroids at us...."

"I doubt it," said Hillory. "He must have used a tremendous amount of psi-power to turn an object moving at super-speed. He probably can't repeat the performance for a long while."

Barton looked relieved. "Then onward and upward to treasure No. 4."

Hillory was guiding the psi-bubble high over earth in a grand arch to the southeast until they swung over Africa at its midsection. Through their clairvoyant goggles set for long range, they spied the snowcapped peak of Kilimanjaro in Tanzania.

"It's eternally cold at its top," marveled Merry, "even though surrounded by equatorial jungles and great tropical heat."

To find the precise point above the mountain, Barton used the Pathfinder to find an imaginary line extending straight up from the peak for 23,500 miles.

"A little more altitude," he said to Hillory. "We're 456 miles below the right level of 23,500 miles. There...that's it. Now two degrees to the west...easy...ah, the satellite should be in sight."

But it wasn't.

They scanned the vicinity with their clairvoyant goggles, which would unerringly pick up anything within a mile. Barton re-read the Pathfinder and had Hillory make minute changes in their altitude and horizontal position until they were exactly above Kilimanjaro's peak beyond question.

Still no object in sight of any kind.

"We're in trouble," growled Barton. "Something must have sent that satellite out of position. Maybe its orbit decayed in 35,000 long years...."

Hillory shook his head. "Up here, six earth radii high, there is no slightest wisp of atmospheric drag to slow an orbiter down. The lifetimes of comsats sent up to this level are estimated as 'eternal' or as long as earth exists."

"A meteoroid could have smashed it head-on," ventured Merry.

"Chances of one in a million," brooded Hillory. "Only a guided meteoroid, like the one Jorzz used, would do the job. It's possible of course, but so highly improbable that it can be discounted."

"Then where *is* the cussed thing?" demanded Barton.

"We're not at the right spot," said Hillory suddenly.

"Man, we're so perfectly over Kilimanjaro's tip that you could drop a stone and hit anybody sitting there."

"Yes, but it's the wrong equator," said Hillory quietly.

"Huh?"

"I get it," said Merry, snapping her fingers. "Theory has it that the earth's axis *changed* in the past, more than once. Fossils of tropical animals and plants have been found in the frozen tundra of the lands near the north pole, for instance. And the discovery of coal in Antarctica proves that jungle forests once grew there."

"Another proof of the earth's axis and therefore its poles changing," added Hillory, "is the famous Piri Reis map which was apparently copied from maps dating back 10,000 years. That map shows the coastline and interior of Antarctica free of ice—only 6,000 or 7,000 years ago"

"A fine kettle of fish," rasped Barton, glaring down at the globe of earth. "The big question is, where were the poles formerly located 35,000 years ago?"

Silence rode in the psi-bubble as three baffled people looked at each other helplessly.

"Let me try something," said Hillory, taking out his tektite crystal. "I'm going to try sending a telepathic message to Brains, the computer. If I can make my thoughts activate its circuit, I can ask a question."

Hillory concentrated then spoke aloud slowly, knowing his telepathic "voice" would also be projected. "Brains! Review all the ancient earth maps we showed you. They're in your memory banks. From them, try to deduce where the north and south geographic poles were 35,000 years ago, and where the line of the equator would run through."

He turned to the others. "A long chance," he confessed.

"You forgot one thing," said Barton disgustedly. "How can you read or hear the answer, if Brains gives it, from some 23,500 miles high plus 7,500 miles northwest?"

For the answer, Hillory adjusted his clairvoyant goggles. The tektite crystal in his hands glowed brighter than ever before, as he siphoned down immense psi-energy. He strained to see and then let out a triumphant yelp.

"I see the screen. It reads—PROBLEM ACCEPTED. SOLVING TIME, 57 SECONDS. A mere brain-teaser to it. All of the ancient maps indicated a shift in polar positions. Some put the former north pole in Asia, others in Africa, and certain other areas on earth. They also marked in estimated temperatures for each region in the world at that time. Brains is apparently confident he can sort out various clues and come to the real solution."

Hillory sent another telepathic command to the computer to give the read-out in lighted words on the screen. A minute later he clairvoyantly read the wording.

AXIS WAS INCLINED 43 DEGREES IN 35,000 B.C. NORTH POLE WAS LOCATED AT WHAT IS NOW SPAIN. SOUTH POLE WAS LOCATED AT NEW ZEALAND. THE EQUATOR THEN RAN THROUGH THE WESTERN UNITED STATES, SOUTHERN TIP OF SOUTH AMERICA, CLOSE TO ANTARCTICA, UP THROUGH THE SOUTH ATLANTIC AND INDIAN OCEANS, AND ACROSS INDIA, CHINA, AND SIBERIA.

Hillory looked confused. "We need a map of the world."

"Right here," said Merry cheerfully, digging it out of their supplies. She spread it, and Hillory drew a penciled line where the old-time equator was.

"But if the equator ran that way," said Barton, baffled, "where is the highest peak in the largest land mass?"

"Simple," said Hillory, but in amazement. "The largest land mass then was Asia as it is now. And the tallest peak was—*Everest.*"

"Everest? That doesn't seem right. Why would the aliens pick the same marker twice?"

"Why not? Mount Everest was unmistakable as the tallest point on earth. They placed one part of the treasure just above the peak, held by a gravity anchor. And they placed another one 23,500 miles higher in a 24-hour orbit, fixed eternally above Everest. And remember, the two treasures are 23,500 miles apart, which is farther apart than any two spots on earth itself. So they aren't 'near' each other by a long shot."

"It all makes sense," agreed Merry. "In fact, it was rather clever of the aliens to hide one treasure at the peak and another in orbit above that same peak. Finding one would give a clue to the other—if you returned in 35,000 B.C. before the equator had changed."

"A clairvoyant search above Mount Everest ought to reveal whether the alien treasure satellite is really there." Hillory was already guiding the psi-bubble away from Africa to the northeast, at a supersonic clip. In a short time they sighted the Himalayas below in which Mount Everest reared grandly.

Barton used the Pathfinder to position them precisely 23,500 miles above the peak. "Now," he said, "suppose we make a spiral sweep around this point. Somewhere we should come across the treasure satellite."

Merry was looking down, wonderingly. "Just to think that 35,000 years ago this was the equator below. All the Himalayas were surrounded by dense tropical jungles. While Spain was the north pole with all of Europe a snowbound arctic land. And New Zealand as the south pole would also make Australia a frozen land."

"America, in turn," added Hillory, "was all part of the equatorial tropics."

"Hey, will you two quit gabbing about the past and look for the alien satellite?" Barton sounded almost annoyed. As if to explain his sharp words he added: "Remember this is No. 4, which will complete the split-up treasure tape. With this one in our hands, we're within reach of solving the whole riddle."

Three pairs of eyes wearing clairvoyant goggles scanned the skies as the psi-bubble made successive sweeps over Mount Everest, in a spiral pattern.

"There she blows," yelled Barton finally, pointing.

A tiny crystal globe hung there in space, glinting in the piercing sunshine. Hillory maneuvered toward it carefully.

"Hold your breaths," he advised. "Or rather, you'll find you lost your breath for a moment."

He briefly opened a flap in the psi-bubble and reached out to yank in the miniature satellite. All the air had whooshed out of the bubble in the meantime, but Barton was already valving fresh oxygen from a tank which quickly filled the interior again. They all took deep breaths.

Then Hillory held up the many-hued crystal globe, which was warm from being in sunlight, rather than cold. "Same contents. The mysterious tape, if it's that."

"Let's hope Dr. Cheng succeeded in opening the others," murmured Merry. She glanced around apprehensively. "And I can bet that Jorzz will be after us again now that he knows we got the fourth treasure globe."

Wasting no time, Hillory sent the psi-bubble scudding to America. He decided to stay high in space where it was unlikely that Jorzz could animate another meteor, leaving him nothing else to play around with.

Finally, over the eastern shoreline of America, Hillory sent the bubble downward. As they descended to 500 miles, they began to see brief streaks of light flashing below them.

"The zone of earth satellites," said Barton. "Over 300 are in orbit today, plus about 2,000 pieces of debris such as burned-out rocket stages and whatnot. Jorzz might try something with those."

Hillory was holding his tektite crystal and concentrating, with a strange trance-like look on his face. Suddenly he said, "Hold on. I'm going to veer sharply past that satellite below."

The bubble would have gone close to the satellite, but now it swung wrenchingly away. A moment later the torpedo-shaped satellite exploded violently, hurling jagged pieces of metal in all directions. The psi-bubble was far enough away to avoid the bomb-burst.

"A Jorzz space-trap," said Hillory, easing back. "When he noticed that that old satellite still had a reserve fuel supply, used for slight orbit changes, he touched off the explosion. It was timed to get us if I hadn't turned the psi-bubble aside."

Barton stared blankly. "But how did you know Jorzz planned to convert us into mincemeat?"

"Precognition," grinned Hillory. "One of the rarer forms of ESP in which you get a glimpse into the future. I saw one minute into the future and knew the satellite was a booby trap waiting for us."

"Seeing into the future," muttered Barton, shaking his head. Suddenly he grabbed Hillory's arm. "Listen, why not work your precognition to see ahead and find out what the tapes are, after the globes are opened. That would save us all of the agony of waiting...."

"Whoa," said Hillory. "It's not that easy. Precognition is one of the hardest and most elusive of psi-phenomena. I really can't control it except for brief moments, like before. Most of the time it won't work as if some sort of 'psi-static' is at work. To choose an exact time in the future, hours or days from now, and to pinpoint what goes on in a certain lab—well, it's simply impossible. I don't have the know-how for that kind of psi-manipulation."

"Oh," said Barton, looking deflated. "Guess we'll have to do it the hard way. Let's hurry back to Serendipity Labs and get cracking."

CHAPTER 17

"*Yes*, the young lady's brilliant idea worked," said Dr. Cheng, pointing at Merry Vedec, who blushed. "By using a wind-tunnel blast of air to hurl one globe against another, they both cracked. The broken pieces showed me that the material wasn't just interlocked atoms but interlocked *protons*."

He turned and pointed at a robot standing motionlessly in the corner. "With that clue, I was able to use a proton-ray and coat steel, creating the indestructible robot!"

"Why did you make a robot indestructible?" asked Hillory curiously.

"As a scientific demonstration piece," said Cheng, "with dramatics. In front of scientists I'll have the robot survive explosions, lasers, fires, cannon shot—everything. That will prove conclusively that Serendipity Labs has produced another science marvel—indestructible matter. It will be parceled out to the world for worthwhile uses only, and not for...."

Hillory was sorry he had asked the question. He cleared his throat. "Yes, yes, Dr. Cheng. But now the treasure tapes. Let's see them."

The dwarfed scientist handed him a box in which lay the coiled-up contents of the three previous crystal globes. "Meanwhile, I'll crack open the fourth globe. Don't worry. I saved a big piece of a broken globe to smash this one open."

Hillory fingered the tape, wonderingly. It uncoiled easily. It looked and felt like common video tape, but on peering closely he saw an intricate pattern of tiny dots all over. Of all different colors, they covered the tapes by the millions or perhaps billions. It was they, sparkling brightly, that had given the crystal globe containers their rainbow hues.

When Cheng had cracked open the fourth crystal globe and handed over the last tape, Hillory strode out with them to Barton's lab.

"Try these on Brains. See if he can make out just what the 'play-back' of this tape will represent."

Barton put one end of a tape under the computer's scanning device with instructions to make a general analysis. The solving time was flashed—98 MINUTES.

Others began to slip into the lab to watch. The word had gone around that the final solution to the alien treasure was close at hand. Practically the whole staff was there, plus Dr. Clyde.

During the 98-minute wait, Hillory was careful to check that everyone had his psi-pistol along, those that had been copied after the one devised for Dr. Torreo's protection. That would ensure that the mind-alien could not pull some psi-animation trick to seize the tapes.

Tension mounted in the room as the time for the computer's answer neared. Merry bit her lips. Barton fiddled with his mustache. Clyde cracked his knuckles. Most everyone else was coughing nervously or brushing invisible lint off his clothes.

Hillory himself felt a strange calm—or was it the calm before a storm? He had a nagging psi-feeling of crisis ahead. Yet he did not know what form it would take. He jerked his body erect when Barton said "time's up" and punched the computer's read-out button for voice.

"The alien tape is not simply to reproduce a voice or a motion picture," said Brains in his usual flat tones. "It is tape of a far greater magnitude that will playback *matter*."

Everyone stiffened in sheer shock. Hillory looked stunned.

"Clarify that," barked Barton.

"The tape would have to be 'played' on a special device that is not known on earth. This device would have access to limitless psi-energy and would follow the code of the tape to convert that energy into solid matter."

Hillory whistled. That was something new to him. Tremendously new.

"What kind of solid matter?" Barton queried of Brains.

"Matter composing a world."

"A world? A whole planet?"

"Yes, but a precise one that once existed but is now only the coding of this matter-tape. Even the living people of that world and their entire civilization would be reproduced."

A concerted gasp arose in the room. Barton almost gagged, so many questions were on his tongue.

"Wait, let's go over this slowly, Brains. That former world no longer exists? What happened to it?"

"I do not know. I can only surmise that it was somehow taken apart or converted into subatomic particles at a certain rate, like a slow explosion. A scanning ray of immense scope then recorded the pattern of that world on tape."

It was mind-staggering, to say the least. In a sense, it was like a video tape transmitting an object line-by-line in swift but perfect detail. But that was only an image broken up into lines and then reassembled as a whole on a screen.

This matter-tape somehow did the incredible and "recorded" the object itself in its physical detail, down to the last atom and meson. And the playback would produce not just an image but the actual world.

Barton had digested the brain-bursting concept and recovered, in a dizzy sort of way. "What is the name of that world?"

"I do not know."

"But I do. Its name was Kaljj!" A new voice, rumbling and scratchy, had answered.

They all whirled as a metallic form marched into the door.

"My robot," exclaimed Dr. Cheng, startled. "How did that iron thing come here…?"

He stopped, and a deathly silence filled the room. Faces paled. They all knew the dread answer.

"Yes," spoke the robot as if reading their minds. "I am Jorzz within this machine. I am here to take away the Tape of Kaljj."

Hillory broke from a frozen trance. "Your psi-pistols," he yelled. "Fire at the robot. It will crumble and force the free-mind of Jorzz to leave."

More than a dozen psi-pistols hissed. They shot at point-blank range. The robot stood with folded arms, mockingly. "You forget that I am Dr. Cheng's *indestructible* robot."

Hillory groaned. Even powerful psi-energy—at least as much as the pistols could handle—could not destroy interlocked protonic matter such as the treasure globes had been made of. It was like trying to blow up the sun with a hydrogen bomb. Everyone shrank back helplessly as the robot strode forward and took all the tapes, stuffing them into a chest cavity that he opened.

The next thought was like a bomb in Hillory's mind. *Jorzz had won*. Nothing could stop him now from using the confiscated tapes and *recreating his home world*. Yes, and *then what…?*

Hillory waved the others back and stepped forward, facing the robot "What are your plans in all this?"

The robot seemed to sneer. "I don't have to answer, of course, earthling. But I want you to be tormented by knowing what will happen—including the conquest of earth itself."

Hillory turned pale. "Go on," he said doggedly.

The robot faced them all as if giving a lecture. "Let me tell you the full history of my world, Kaljj. It was a living world more than 35,000 of your earth years ago. I was Jorzz, the Star King. My world reached an acme of technological might and swept out conquering worlds to form a star empire of my own. What great forces and weapons we used I will not attempt to describe."

Hillory shuddered. He did not want to know.

The words rang on, lifting a corner of the curtain that hid galactic history from earth's unknowing eyes. "The Galactic Union did not like my doings. They had ruled the galaxy for a million years, as a union of free planets. They had outlawed campaigns of conquest and empire building. Their spaceships patrolled the galaxy to keep law and order, as they called it. I knew they would attack me and I was prepared—I thought."

Jorzz paused as if tasting the bitterness of defeat again. Then his robot voice resumed. "What I did not know was that they had devised a secret weapon more powerful than any known before—the space shaker. It was some amazing force that could *shake space*. I cannot describe it any more clearly to your limited earth minds. The result was that my invincible space armada was no longer invincible. My ships were literally shaken to pieces as the space around them vibrated powerfully."

Subtle agony seemed to come through the automaton's voice, as it went on.

"The GU patrol ships then surrounded my planet and condemned our whole world to the maximum penalty of *non-death*. I will have to explain. The death penalty for any crime, by individuals or worlds, had been abolished. Yet the guilty one could be 'destroyed' without being destroyed. Briefly, a modification of the space-shaker ray shook my world to bits in an orderly pattern and the matter-tape recorder coded it all down meticulously—buildings, people, animals, the ground, the entire planet. It was painless and swift with a scanning rate that finished the job in a trifle under one second."

Hillory's mind reeled, trying to take in these concepts a macro-magnitude beyond earthly science. But then, it was just an extension of the super-speed scanning utilized in TV to hurl images to the receiver at the speed of light.

"And so Kaljj was destroyed and recorded on tape," said the robot. "But at any time the tape could be used to reproduce my world again, down to the last atom. The people would live again with their former memories, just as real as they were before. They would simply be made of new matter."

It was awesome, fantastic, incomprehensible. But that was only to the human mind, Hillory knew, not the galactic mind with a background of a million years of super-science.

Jorzz went on, via the robot's mechanical voice.

"The GU's plan was to store the tapes for a specified sentence of what would be approximately 1,000 earth years. At that time, it would replay the tape and recreate our world to live again. But in that time my former empire would have been broken up, rehabilitated, and armed to resist any further attack from me. And Kaljj would be allowed to enter the GU councils with only a half vote for another thousand years, until they had proved they could take their place as a civilized, law-abiding world."

Hillory was still puzzled. "How do you fit into all this? Why are you not part of that tape?"

The robot eyed him. "As the Star King, leader of conquest for a star empire, my sentence was to be taped for *five thousand* years, by myself, so that when I returned even my people wouldn't know me. They would have a different government entirely."

Very effective, thought Hillory, admiringly. The Galactic Union leaders sagaciously dealt in sweeping cosmic terms and knew how to be stern and merciful at the same time.

"But I escaped," boomed the robot proudly. "My scientists had been dabbling with psi-phenomena, and they had made ready a device for separating the psyche from the body or the mind from the brain. It was untried, admittedly dangerous, and might not work. It was a gamble I had to take. Just before my world was disintegrated and taped, I stepped in the device, a super centrifuge. The theory was that if my body were whirled at an almost inconceivable speed, it would hurl out my free mind. You of course know how centrifuges separate things of different density. The mind, being of comparatively low density, was flung out of my dense body…it had worked."

Jorzz paused as if to collect his thoughts.

"I found myself invisible, wafting away from my planet into open space, at will. I did not need air or food, only energy from any sun or star, which I absorbed. Experimenting, I found I had certain psi-powers, such as the ability to animate objects—as you well know."

Hillory grunted at the implied sarcasm. He spoke up. "But how did the tape ever get on earth, split up into four parts?"

"That goes into another story that I pieced together after the event. A band of space pirates knew that the Kaljj tape was stored in the underground vaults of the GU. They made a daring raid and snatched the tape away."

"What was their aim?" Hillory inquired.

"Their aim was to play the tape and recreate Kaljj, and then *rule* it. They knew I had been disposed—or thought so, not knowing of my escape as a free-mind. But they knew the space patrol would hound them relentlessly after this major theft, so they had to let things quiet down. In their spaceship they then searched for a small, obscure world, one not even marked on the GU charts. Earth was their choice. They split the tape and buried it in four unique places, then made the metal scroll map so they could find the treasure again. Their plan was to return in ten years and pick up the tape when they were no longer marked men. As further crimes and coups occurred to occupy the patrol, their crime receded in importance."

They would no longer be space enemies number one, translated Hillory. The heat would be off, and they could dig up their treasure and enjoy the reward. A crime of macrocosmic scope but still essentially no different from similar piratical practices on earth all through history.

"But as I briefly explained once before," resumed Jorzz, "the pirates were apprehended before the ten years were up. They put up a fight and had to be killed—all except one, who slipped away in a flying saucer lifeboat. He had the metal map along and came to earth to retrieve the four-part treasure himself. The rest you know."

That pirate's saucer craft had crashed on earth, to be found that vital day by Hillory and Merry.

The robot now swiveled its eyes around at the company.

"I told you that when Kaljj is created and starts empire building again, earth will be one of its conquests. Not only that, but the playback machine will be built right here on earth—by Serendipity Labs."

CHAPTER 18

A gasp of horror filled the room. Hillory writhed inwardly at this culmination of their treasure hunt. The treasure they had unearthed was hardly something valuable. It was instead something of frightful menace not only to earth but to a million other worlds. Hillory could see now why the mind-alien had hounded them so mercilessly for the prize which would be the revival of Jorzz's world and mad career.

A thought struck Hillory. To the robot he said, "But if you're a free mind, a disembodied mind, you won't return to life with a body, as your people will."

"Ah, but I will. When my mind had been centrifuged from my body, my mindless body remained on Kaljj. It was not lifeless. And when Kaljj was taped into non-death, my body was included. Thus, when Kaljj is recreated, my living body will be waiting for me."

Hillory sagged. Jorzz had thought of everything. Yet maybe not. "If the Galactic Union's space patrol defeated you last time with the space-shaker weapon, how can you oppose them a second time?"

A gleam seemed to come into the robot's eye-lenses. "But I will have a greater weapon than the space-shaker. Remember that I drifted through the universe for 35,000 years as a free mind. Besides tracking down the story of the space pirates who stole and hid the tape, I had time to dabble in science, using telepathy to read the minds of great galactic scientists. One of them had studied the secrets of time and came close to a great discovery. He did not carry out the last step in his calculations, but I did. Then it sprang into my mind—the *time-shaker* weapon. It is greater than the space-shaker weapon."

Jorzz went on almost fiendishly with his robot larynx.

"The space-shaker takes time to vibrate a warship and disintegrate it. But the time-shaker will work instantly. It will send the space patrol ships to the end of infinity, or into oblivion, all in the wink of an eye. My ships will easily wipe out the GU space patrol fleet. Then the entire galactic universe and its millions of civilized worlds will become the Star Empire of Jorzz."

Hillory's mind reeled. His treasure hunt had unwittingly unleashed an intelligent monster upon the universe. Human he might be in form when he regained his body, but mentally he was a super-tyrant, power-hungry to rule billions and trillions of people on millions of worlds. No Alexander nor Napoleon nor Hitler on earth had ever had such grandiose ambitions. The worst of it was that with his super-science knowledge, Jorzz could attain his goals and browbeat a whole galaxy.

But first he had to browbeat the members of Serendipity Labs—if he could. "How will you get us to help you and make the tape playback machine?" said Hillory defiantly. "If you're thinking of hypnotism, you know it didn't work too successfully. The spell can be broken. How else can you get us to do your dirty work, if we refuse? Threatening to kill us won't work either, for killing us is the last thing you want."

Yet even as he said it, Hillory had the sinking feeling that Jorzz had figured out some psi-plan to coerce them. His hunch was right.

The robot first took a tektite crystal from its chest storage space. At Hillory's startled glance he said: "Stole it from your lab. Now to draw down psi-energy and...."

A moment later, Hillory felt the stab of psi-power in his mind. He yawned, suddenly feeling sleepy. Around him, the others all exhibited signs of weariness, and some lay down on the floor. Warning leaped into Hillory's mind.

"Fight it," he yelled. "Fight the desire to sleep or...ahhh..."

Yawning prodigiously, Hillory was unable to go on. Nobody could fight the powerful urge to sleep. "You see?" said the robot triumphantly. "I've used another portion of your psi-chart—*dreams*. That is, my psi-projection is putting everyone to sleep in a dreaming state."

It was true. Everyone else had succumbed to the overwhelming craving for sleep and lay on the floor. Only Hillory was still standing, trying to fight it off, but swaying on his feet.

To him the robot said, "The significant part of the dream state is *somnambulism*. Watch what happens at my mental command now—ARISE! ARISE AND OBEY MY INSTRUCTIONS."

Hillory saw them all struggle to their feet, eyes closed, still asleep. But now they became sleepwalkers as Jorzz ordered them around the room. It was like a psi-drug, more powerful than any tranquilizing drug. They were like zombies with no will of their own. It was, Hillory realized, the step beyond hypnotism, placing the subject completely under the control of Jorzz.

The robot eyed Hillory, who still was not fully in a somnambulistic state and did not join the others marching aimlessly in the room. "Only you, with your psi-practice, are still defiant. Hmm, if you do not become completely somnambulistic in a few more seconds...."

Warning lanced into Hillory's mind. He was expendable. If he remained free of Jorzz's control, the mind-alien would consider him a menace and crush him in the robot's powerful arms. Hillory let his head droop and his eyes close. Slowly he shuffled his feet and joined the other sleepwalkers going in a circle.

"Ah, even he succumbed at last," crowed the robot. He held up a hand. "Attention, all of you. You will now each return to your labs. I will give you instructions what to do. You will be making parts for the planet playback tape that will recreate my world, Kaljj. But you will open your eyes and act alert, so that if any visitors come, they will think you are merely working on your own experiments, as before. If they ask questions, you will answer normally. You will say nothing about the treasure tapes, or Jorzz, or the playback machine. Understand?"

They all snapped their eyes open and nodded.

"Good. And the visitors will never suspect that the robot they see standing motionlessly is really the psi-master of Serendipity Labs, working toward his goal of the second Star Empire. Now go."

Obediently they left, but acting quite alert, not looking at all like somnambulists in a deep sleep. Hillory left with them, filled with black despair. There seemed no way to stop Jorzz. By animating the indestructible robot, Jorzz was invulnerable to attack. Even if the army came, their biggest guns would not destroy his impervious form. Dr. Cheng could not be wrong on that score. So what good would it do for Hillory to escape and inform the authorities? Inform them that even nuclear bombs could not wreck the robot?

And no psi-powers either could finish off the robot, at least none that Hillory could bring to bear. It would take a hundred psi-experts perhaps, drawing down psi-energy from the universal pool, to project a psi-blast powerful enough to smash the interlocked protonic matter of the robot's body.

Hopeless. Hillory went back to his lab. By using his clairvoyant goggles, he was able to see the robot going from lab to lab and handing out blueprints for them to work on. The blueprints of the playback machine that would recreate Kaljj, world of tyranny. And create havoc in the universe.

But how would it work, the machine? As if in answer to his question, the robot stumped into Hillory's lab.

"Listen, my psi-slave," chortled Jorzz, "you cannot make any mechanical parts of my machine, but you will be useful later for forming a huge psi-levitation bubble to transport the machine into space. You will guide it into an orbit around your sun, between the orbits of Venus and Earth. There, the tape will be automatically fed into the playback machine which will tap the universal psi-pool for immense amounts of psi-energy. That energy will be converted into matter which will follow the tape's coding and fashion the world Kaljj."

Hillory wanted to ask a question but didn't dare. A somnambulist did not speak but only listened and obeyed. However, Jorzz wanted to get Hillory's later job clear and answered his unvoiced question.

"Yes, Kaljj will remain in your solar system, which I will adopt. When my armadas are ready, they will first come and take over earth. Quite an honor, you know, for your world to be the first member of my new Star Empire."

A scathing remark surged into Hillory's mind, and he suppressed it with an effort. But he also shuddered at the coming fate of earth.

"Don't worry," mocked Jorzz as if to be soothing. "Earth will not suffer much disaster. Your military forces will be defeated in a short time, and the world will be taken over with hardly a shot fired. That ought to comfort you."

Hillory writhed, trembling in his effort to keep from blurting out his scorn and hatred for this vile mind-entity.

The robot patted Hillory on the back, less than gently.

"I am not even angry with you for opposing me during the treasure hunt and evading all my clever psi-tricks. After earth is mine,

I might even make you my Master of Psionics to teach my people your psi-powers. Does that please you?"

Only superhuman will kept Hillory from grabbing up a tool and smashing it in the robot's face, behind which leered the invisible mind-alien who had things all his own way now.

Humiliated, Hillory said or did nothing as the robot strode out. Once alone, Hillory pounded his fist into the wall till his knuckles were bruised. Then he slumped into a chair in abject frustration. He felt like crying and almost did.

The most hideous part of the whole deal was that he—Hillory—had been chosen for the "honor" of psi-levitating the playback machine into space for its Machiavellian task. Hillory would be launching the mind-alien's whole horrendous plot into the universe.

Hillory could not cry. But he could groan in super-misery.

* * * *

A month went by. No news leaked to the outside world as to the horror going on in Serendipity Labs. When supply trucks came, or visiting scientists dropped by, all seemed normal. The somnambulistic staff were well schooled by Jorzz to act normally, creating no suspicion.

Dr. Clyde also acted his part, guiding visiting officials around and explaining each scientist's researches—his former researches. The innocent-looking parts for the playback machine were ignored.

Hillory also kept mum when outsiders came. What use to tell them? What good to let the government or the world know about Jorzz's plan—if they could not destroy the robot? Even if they destroyed the robot, Jorzz's free mind would waft away with the psi-towed tapes and start his project all over again on some other world. One thought kept going like a squirrel-cage in his mind—*Jorzz would have to be stopped right here in Serendipity Labs, or not at all.* There must be *some* way to circumvent him, Hillory kept telling himself every day. But a dozen schemes bubbled up in his mind only to be discarded. An indestructible robot plus a super-scientific free-mind…it was a formidable combination whose defeat seemed almost inconceivable.

In one big engineering lab, the playback machine began to take shape under the hands of Jorzz's somnambulistic slaves. Hillory was rather surprised at its unimposing appearance. It was no more than the size of a computer cabinet. But then, the machine did not have to be some giant complex just because it would perform the giant task of "replaying" a world and making it materialize out of nothingness. It would be the boundless input of psi-power that would do the real job. The machine was only a relay and guidance system for those mighty forces.

Intricate parts went into the playback cabinet.

Hillory winced as he saw his colleagues troop in one by one and add a part. They had fixed stares and did not even greet each other.

Alloway Argyle, with his pirate's black eye patch, came in and fitted a radioactive scanner to the machine. Allen Chumley attached servo-mechanisms that looked like human hands, based on his android work. Ivan Yonah contributed a timing device without saying a word, not even a cussword. Dr. Cheng fastened shielding plates into place, perhaps made of indestructible matter. Dr. Spindle hooked up some sort of organic growth in a sealed glass globe which might trigger the playback circuit into recreating human beings. Dr. Torreo put in a dimension probe which would probably play some eerie part in this materialization of a world out of limbo.

Jim Barton too was a vital part of the project, running complex equations and data through Brains, integrating all the functions of the playback machine. Barton, as Hillory looked in sadly through his clairvoyant goggles, no longer twirled his handlebar mustache. He worked with a dead face and expressionless eyes, like a human robot.

And Merry Vedec. Hillory felt most pained as he watched her and the other girl technicians laboriously putting microminiaturized circuits together. Merry's eyes were watery from the exacting work with tiny things. She didn't smile when Hillory walked in one day and impulsively leaned over and kissed her. She glanced at him as if he didn't exist. Then she went back somnambulistically to her work under the orders of Jorzz to never rest.

The psi-slaves were allowed to eat and sleep. At night they simply went from a sleepwalking state to a bed-resting state without "waking up" at all. They were caught in the dreamlike psi-trap of the mind-alien, living a nightmare.

CHAPTER 19

Doomed, doomed. All of them. And all earth. And all the known universe. The terrifying words boomed constantly through Hillory's aching mind. A month—and he hadn't yet come anywhere near a plan to defeat Jorzz. Maybe there was no way....

Hillory began to feel like a somnambulist himself. He didn't have to act when the robot came in his lab. Day after day Hillory worked with his new tektite "crown", decorated with a dozen of his largest specimens. He practiced the technique of siphoning down psi-energy from a dozen different tektites. He would need enormous psi-levitation power to create the psi-bubble Jorzz had demanded. And he would need the multi-psi crown to propel the playback machine for millions of miles, to its own solar orbit where the world Kaljj would be conjured out of nothingness into reality.

Lift...lift...lift up and float. Hillory beamed his ESP forces at a heavy weight, equal to the playback machine, in a psi-bubble. It rose tentatively an inch, then thudded back. Hillory did not want it to work, but he knew it would, when the time came. He had carried on his research because he couldn't afford not to. He had to pretend to play ball with Jorzz, while his whirling thoughts kept seeking for the way to crush him.

Lift...float...don't act like something super-heavy that...." Hillory's whole mind seemed to light up at that lightning-flash thought. *Super-heaviness*, the opposite of levitation. The golden key.

* * * *

"Has your levitation power reached the proper level?" The robot glowered at Hillory. "Give me a demonstration."

With a wooden face, Hillory put on the tektite-crown with its dozen crystals that flashed all dazzling colors of the rainbow. Jorzz did not notice Hillory's eyes shifting and focusing on the robot form itself.

Then, summoning all the psi-energy pouring down through the twelve tektites, Hillory boomed out silent telepathic commands— ROBOT! TURN SUPER-HEAVY…HEAVIER THAN LEAD…A HUNDRED TIMES HEAVIER THAN LEAD. THE FORCE OF GRAVITY IS DOING IT…DOUBLING AND TRIPLING UNDER YOU AND MULTIPLYING CONSTANTLY…SINK…*SINK*!

The words were meaningless, merely a focal point for what he really projected—a psi-force that would intensify gravity under the robot to a fantastic degree.

Within the robot, Jorzz was startled and caught unaware. "Sabotage," he yelled. "I'll crush you, Hillory…."

But as the robot tried to step forward, its foot smashed through the floor as if it were paper. The whole body of the robot then ripped down through the floor—and kept going. It sank into hard ground as if it were cheese. When it struck rock, it plunged right through it without stopping. Its speed downward increased.

Looking down the hole, Hillory yelled telepathically, "Having fun, Jorzz? Your robot body is being yanked down by 100 g's of force. In effect, it's like a dense chunk of lead sinking through syrup. That indestructible form will keep going down…down…to the center of the earth, 4,000 miles below. That's a trap you can't rescue your robot body from, no matter how you try."

Hillory picked up Jorzz's faint telepathic cries from a mile down. "Rise! Rise, you clumsy thing…stop sinking…rise."

Jorzz was putting all his psi-power into it, but it could never counteract the immense psi-energy Hillory had piled up with his dozen tektite "pumps". It was a losing battle—for the mind-alien.

With a telepathic curse, Jorzz gave up. Hillory knew that his free mind had abandoned the sinking robot form, now ten miles down and going at almost rocket speed through the crust of earth, heading for its final eternal haven at the planet's center where zero-g existed.

Hillory had separated Jorzz from his steel fortress. A big step. But the next step was even more vital. Hillory again drew down power through the psi-crystals, frantically increasing it to a flood.

Then, holding his breath, he gave the verbal command that would be translated in some subtle manner into psi-action—SEPARATE MY MIND FROM MY BODY…MAKE ME A FREE MIND… NOW!

Instant pain shot through Hillory's head. An intense pain beyond description. He felt as if some great tongs were yanking and trying to pull his brain out by the roots. But he knew what it was—psi-forces severing the tight bond between his mind and the host body it was born into. And clung to, stubbornly.

Hillory now felt as if he—his mental self—were being stretched out like a rubber band. The agony went beyond his sense of feeling, like a sound rising in pitch beyond the human ear. He felt nothing now except the ferocious tugging force.

Then suddenly there was a silent *whung* like a rubber band snapping loose. Hillory's senses blacked out—hearing, sight, smell, taste, feeling. But to his amazement, he was now "seeing" more clearly than ever before. And "hearing" with extraordinary sharpness. Extrasensory perception…ESP…was his, unimpeded.

Though prepared, it gave him a little shock to see his body—his physical body—lying inert on the floor, the tektite crown askew. The body looked dead, lifeless. But Hillory knew that its life processes were merely suspended.

But the real Hillory—his mental identity—was hanging in mid-air in the lab, as if divorced entirely from the pull of gravity. To his astonishment, Hillory looked down and saw that he still had a body—a wraithlike naked body—exactly like his material body.

Fleetingly, he thought how this followed the paranormal thesis that within the human body existed an exact formfitting "astral body" which was infinitely less dense than living flesh. Paired throughout life, these two "bodies" separated at death—but there was no death really. The astral form, the real person, lived on.…

Hillory shook those thoughts away. No time now to speculate on those lofty, soul-shaking concepts. He had a job to do. He was now a free mind and could *battle* the free mind of Jorzz, on equal terms.

He tensed and swam a bit through the air as he heard a rushing sound from below and then an ectoplasmic form shot up through the hole in the floor that the robot had made.

For the first time, with his psychic eyes, Hillory saw his enemy in human form, a wraithlike duplicate of his living form. Big and broad-shouldered, Jorzz had thick arms and legs. His short neck supported a broad head with fleshy lips, a jutting chin, and two coal-black eyes that burned in towering rage.

A telepathic hiss came from the alien. "You have ruined my present plans, earthling. For this I shall destroy you. I'll draw down great psi-forces and blast you into oblivion."

Jorzz pointed his finger and a chain of sparkles extended through the air between them touching Hillory and making him tingle all over agonizingly. Hillory realized it was some strange form of psi-electricity that could electrocute him in his pure-mind form.

Hillory was also drawing down psi-energy from the universal pool and found he could now do it without the tektite crystals. He hastily erected a ghost-like shield in front of him that warded off the livid sparks.

"Two can play this game, Jorzz," said Hillory grimly, and at the same time he used psi-force to hurl the shield at his enemy. It struck him quite like a steel shield would and hurled him back.

Jorzz recovered and snarled. Then he suddenly changed his form into that of a towering monster with long tentacles. This was a complete surprise to Hillory, not knowing of the eerie powers of a pure-mind entity. The tentacles lashed forth and whipped around him, squeezing ferociously. Hillory did not feel his breath gasping out—he had no breath. But he could feel his psi-body being slowly crushed. Something akin to having his body mangled would result, and the ending would be death to his mental form.

Struggling desperately, Hillory willed himself to turn into a serpentine form, which he instantly did. He was then able to wriggle out of the monsters clutches.

They both snapped back to their psi-forms, and Hillory stood for a moment dizzy from the mauling he had received.

"Ah, you are weakened," gloated Jorzz, quickly forming a huge ectoplasmic hand that rammed forward and clipped Hillory on his chin, knocking him off his feet. As Jorzz came rushing at him with an ectoplasmic spear, Hillory realized he had to act fast.

Summoning up psi-energy, Hillory improvised on the spur of the moment and created a dazzling globe of blinding light. Unable to see momentarily, Jorzz stumbled and thrust wildly with his spear, missing Hillory by a wide margin.

The blinding ball and spear vanished quickly. Such ectoplasmic or psi-formed phenomena could not be sustained for more than a short time. Hillory saw that he was at a disadvantage. The pure-mind state was entirely new to him, whereas Jorzz had experienced it for thousands of years and knew what weird manifestations he could produce. Hillory would have to use his wits and second-guess his enemy until he felt more confident in his new role.

Hillory also knew that none of this could be seen or heard by anyone in Serendipity Labs. The human eye was blind to such psychic activity. It was like two ghosts battling, having no material effect on their surroundings. No furniture would be smashed or windows broken. It was all taking place on the etheric plane, divorced from the earth plane, though they could see everything around them.

Jorzz stood blinking to clear his eyes, after the blinding light. "Clever, earthling," he conceded. "But you have no idea of the many psi-tricks I can use. And here they come, faster than you can avoid them…."

Twin beams of a peculiar color shot from Jorzz's eyes, turning into a stream of steely daggers aimed straight at Hillory's heart. Hillory instantly folded his flexible body at the hips in a right-angle and bent backwards. The daggers spun over him and faded.

Flashingly, Hillory saw his only hope—to make Jorzz use up his psi-energy reserves as fast as possible. So Hillory willed himself to flit up in the air. He oozed through the lab building's roof as if it weren't there and soared into the sky.

"Coward," yelled Jorzz, in hot pursuit. "My barrage will still get you."

Jorzz began hurling forth an assortment of deadly things—spinning saw-blades, spiked clubs, axes and hatchets, even bombs and missiles. Though modeled after material weapons, they were made of psi-matter and could quite definitely wound Hillory if they struck him.

Flying through the air, Hillory dodged wildly. Queer, how the astral body inherited many of the physical body's attributes, such as reflexes. Hillory relied on them to escape Jorzz's barrage of death.

But as a buzz-saw blade whistled narrowly past his ear, Hillory desperately flew down into a mountain, penetrating through its rock, hoping to lose himself from his relentless pursuer.

"Fool. I simply switch on clairvoyant vision," roared Jorzz. Twin beams shot from Jorzz's eyes, and he kept on Hillory's heels through the solid stone. Hillory knew he could hide nowhere from that psi-sight, nowhere on earth. How about space?

Hillory shot himself upward at mounting speed, straight toward the moon. The mind-alien's hoarse cry sounded behind him. "I'll follow you to the moon, the planets, the stars. You cannot escape me anywhere in the universe."

And in open space, Hillory stood out as a clear target so that a psi-arrow clipped his shoulder. In panic, Hillory turned down toward earth again and plunged into thick clouds, which momentarily hindered Jorzz until he focused his clairvoyant vision.

It was a grim and deadly chase as they sped back to earth. Hillory began to feel like the hunted rabbit or fox. How could he elude the vengeful alien? Hillory did not dare turn and meet him face to face—not yet. He did not know how to handle his astral form and psi-powers adequately in comparison to Jorzz's psi-skills.

But the chase could not go on forever. He had to think of something quickly, something to turn the tables, to take Jorzz by surprise. Keeping his eyes turned backward, Hillory saw Jorzz hurl a bomb with a burning fuse. Inspiration leaped into Hillory s mind. He turned swiftly to meet the bomb and catch it, hurling it back.

It did not reach Jorzz, but it exploded near him and surrounded him with thick smoke. When the smoke cleared before the alien's eyes, Hillory was gone.

Jorzz looked around, bewildered. "Where are you, coward?" he bellowed. "But you can't hide from my clairvoyant vision." Jorzz swung his eyes from side to side, scanning all areas ahead. But he saw nothing of his quarry. Puzzled, Jorzz began to walk forward, searching in all directions.

Directly behind Jorzz moved his shadow. But it was a peculiar shadow that walked upright on the ground. Besides, a pure-mind entity had no shadow.

Hillory grinned a bit to himself, at the simple trick he had pulled. While the bomb smoke had momentarily obscured the alien's vision, Hillory had swiftly leaped behind Jorzz and darkened his skin to look like a shadow. Even if Jorzz caught a glimpse of him through the corner of his eye, he would take it for some kind of shadow of something.

Hillory followed the mind-alien's footsteps precisely to keep from being detected. Jorzz was becoming more and more baffled, as Hillory could see by the way he rapped his knuckles against his head at times.

And this gave Hillory time to gather in potent amounts of psi-energy. Hillory finally used it to expand his hands to triple their size. Then he banged one oversized fist against the back of the alien's head, stunning him.

Jorzz lurched around, in shocked surprise.

"I was right behind you all the time," mocked Hillory, at the same time going into a boxer's stance and slamming his huge fists into the alien's face. "Better not try conjuring up weapons, Jorzz. Conserve your psi-power, what you have left, to defend yourself. This is the earth style of man-to-man fighting. Put up your dukes, as we say."

All the while Hillory was battering Jorzz. The alien saw he had no choice and tried to strike back, but kept missing the one-time college boxing champ. Odd, thought Hillory fleetingly, that it should all end up this way—in a common brawl. Two mind-entities battling it out with etheric fists.

But the etheric blows counted against an etheric chin. With savage joy, Hillory pounded away, reducing Jorzz to a staggering mass of bruises. Any referee would have called the match as being sheer slaughter. But Hillory's referee was his own rage.

"Recreate your evil world, eh? Have a left to the jaw. Conquer earth? A nice uppercut. Enslave the universe like a mad dog? Here's the knockout."

One last blow, with all of Hillory's psi-power behind it, flattened Jorzz. He groaned a little, then lay sprawled. Hillory sat down, his head on his knees, spent.

Too late he saw the alien stir, then leap erect. Hillory realized, bitterly, that Jorzz had faked being knocked out. And now it was Hillory in pursuit as the alien sped purposefully through the air, toward Serendipity Labs.

When Hillory caught up, he saw Jorzz flitting into one of the androids in Dr. Chumley's lab. Hillory tried to grab the android, but his hands passed through. Cursing at forgetting his astral state, Hillory wafted himself to his own lab and oozed back into his inert body.

He felt a sort of shock as his physical and mental forms interlocked again.

Then he arose, once more in human form. He raced down the hall and saw the android in the computer lab, gathering up all the treasure tapes. Hillory stopped dead as the android held up a peculiar weapon.

"The time-shaker gun," said Jorzz through the android's lips. "The engineers finished the test model for me. Now a psi-bubble will waft me away from earth with the Kaljj tape. On some other world I can still take over control of scientists and have them build the playback machine. So my second Star Empire is only delayed in its debut. I win after all. As for you, earthling, be prepared to be puffed into eternity...."

Barton and Merry were in the doorway, staring in horror. They had snapped out of their somnambulistic trance when the battle between Hillory and Jorzz had begun, with Jorzz unable to keep feeding psi-energy into the mental spell he held over them.

With a mocking laugh that came from Jorzz, the android pressed the trigger-stud. There was a soundless puff....

But Hillory still stood there. The android had vanished.

An engineer came dashing in. "Jorzz didn't know he was pointing the time-shaker gun the wrong way. He was aiming it at himself."

"Ridiculous," cried Merry Vedec, laughing hysterically, "How could the greatest menace in the universe be wiped out that easily, by his own stupid doing?"

Hillory stared around at the others with a strange glint in his eyes. "An incredible blunder like that could only happen because of one thing..." He didn't have to tell them the word....

Serendipity.

www.ingramcontent.com/pod-product-compliance
Lightning Source LLC
Chambersburg PA
CBHW020656180626
46816CB00003B/1307